I0775064

MALVINA TAPLEY

Lit by Stars

First published by Malvina Tapley 2025

Copyright © 2025 by Malvina Tapley

All rights reserved. No part of this publication may be reproduced, stored or transmitted in any form or by any means, electronic, mechanical, photocopying, recording, scanning, or otherwise without written permission from the publisher. It is illegal to copy this book, post it to a website, or distribute it by any other means without permission.

This novel is entirely a work of fiction. The names, characters and incidents portrayed in it are the work of the author's imagination. Any resemblance to actual persons, living or dead, events or localities is entirely coincidental.

First edition

ISBN (paperback): 978-1-969114-00-7
ISBN (hardcover): 978-1-969114-02-1

This book was professionally typeset on Reedsy.
Find out more at reedsy.com

To all the stories ever told—
And to the storytellers, who found the words.

Chapter One

She sat still, staring out into the night, remembering. The sky over the desert was lit by countless thousands of stars. The silver crescent of a new moon shed its own soft radiance over the sand. The night was cool, and she shivered a little. But she did not feel the desert breeze: rather, a harsher wind from her memory. Instead of the ocean of sand, faintly visible in the moonlight and starlight, she seemed to see another ocean, one of salt water and rolling waves. For a moment, she thought she could smell the salt and the brine in the air, hear the shouts of the fishermen as they unloaded the boats.

The remembered sea and the sand before her alike gave way to other images. The towering, silent trees of a forest far away, a long walk in the springtime. A dusty road in the first heat of summer, with the smell of crushed ragweed and drying hay filling the air. Hard stone walls, a narrow cell, air that was close and hot, yet never escaped a faint chill. Other walls, in a spacious room, the stone this time almost hidden by rich rugs and tapestries. An endless walk through a night of pouring rain. A journey up a mountain in the autumn. She gazed out over the sand, remembering...

Echo was born in a small village beside a great sea. The inhabitants and their ancestors had been there for time out of mind, fighting for a living from the stubborn earth and the pitiless sea. Stubborn as the earth, as indomitable as the sea, fiercely proud of their heritage and way of life, they were yet kindhearted and good-humored. Closeknit but independent, each stood on his own two feet but stood always ready to help his neighbor. Equally ready to laugh or to fight, to work or to feast as the occasion called, they were in all the kind of people that are the salt of the earth.

Such was Echo's heritage. These were her people, her place in the world, the land and sea that her ancestors had belonged to for uncounted generations. She loved her village, but she was never truly part of it.

Echo was a teller of stories. Stories were as real to her as the real world. All the stories she knew were a part of her, as she was part of them. She knew more than a thousand stories. She lived in more than a thousand different worlds.

Stories have power, the power to make a person laugh or cry, shiver or smile. A well-told story can make a person feel, change a person's mind, give someone a whole new point of view. Each tale has something to tell, a history to relate, a lesson to be learned. Stories hold whole lives, whole lifetimes, the wisdom of ages, and endless knowledge. Contained in stories there is good and evil, joy and sadness, love and hate, triumph and disaster, humor and tragedy, wit and foolishness, and humdrum and every-day happenings. In fact, all the happiness and woe, strangeness and ordinariness of human existence.

Stories hold the power of all the things contained in them. Echo knew more than a thousand stories, and she knew their power. This knowledge set her apart from her people.

Where does any story truly begin? Echo wondered. And what story can be said to have ended? Had her story begun the day she left her village? The day she was born? Perhaps far earlier, the day her grandfather had left the same village? Or the day he had returned to it? Stories were tangled, one blending into another in a complicated web of knowledge and experiences. To begin at the beginning was nearly impossible, because even beginnings had their root in things that happened long ago. And even after a story was ended, the consequences of its happenings could change the course of another story. A circle, thought Echo. More than that, many circles, twisted in an ever-changing pattern that looks incredibly complicated, but can sometimes, by a few, be seen from a great distance. Then she laughed at herself a little. *No matter how much we think we see, or how clear it looks, we still only see a tiny piece of the whole picture. No storyteller can tell more than a piece of it.* She thought again of the village by the sea where she had lived for most of her life. She had been there when things had begun for her.

* * *

Echo danced barefoot over the freshly plowed ground, full of life and the joy of living. The worst thing about winter, she decided, was undoubtedly the necessity for shoes. But now it was the spring of the year, and shoes could be discarded, along with heavy cloaks, hats, gloves, and all the restrictive trappings of cold weather. Food would be easier to come by again; no one would have to worry about going hungry for another eight months. Birds were singing, not just in the morning, but all the day through. Their music could be heard from morning till noon till night, in a never-ending song of spring. Everything was growing, awakening, and it was wonderful just to be alive, the kind of day where you want to dance and sing for sheer joy...

Echo was beautiful, with an odd, outlandish sort of loveliness. Even her looks were unusual, set her apart. She was of medium height, slender, but sturdy. Her hair was a dark, smoke black, very fine and straight and usually blowing out around her head like a cloud. Her mouth was wide, with a quirk of amusement that rarely left it even when her eyes were serious. But it was her eyes that truly added the oddity to her beauty. They were a warm, light brown, with yellow flecks that made them look gold.

She stood in a small field, squarish in shape, surrounded on three sides by trees. It had been carved from the forest, the trees hewed down and used for building, the stumps laboriously removed to make a space that could be used for growing the food necessary to feed a family through the winter. The forest did not give up easily, however. Each year, roots reached a little farther into the field, and young trees sprang up in the place of the old ones that had been cut down. And each year the farmers, as stubborn as the trees, pushed the forest back again. The fourth side of the field was marked by a low hedge, over which could be seen the thatched roofs of the village of Pebblestone, and beyond them a glimpse of the sea. The field had been plowed the day before, and Echo should really not have been dancing on it. Her feet packed the ground, which would make it more difficult to plant in.

The crumbly surface of the freshly turned earth was warm from the sun, but the hard ground beneath was still cold from winter. The air also felt pleasantly warm after the cold of winter, but it was only an illusion. It would not be truly hot for some time yet. The sky was that clear, cloudless blue peculiar to early spring. Echo spun, soaking up the feeling of the earth under her feet, the sun warm on her face. She stretched her arms to their fullest extent as she whirled around, her feet flying over the ground, her hair flying out in a cloud around her head. She did not sing aloud, but in her mind one word was repeated like a song. Joyous, joyous, joyous. It seemed to Echo the most perfect description of spring in a single word.

A woman stepped into the field, carrying a box and followed by a laughing child with hair the color of sunshine. Echo caught a glimpse of the motion through the whirling world about her and stopped spinning abruptly. She picked up the hoe that she had dropped a few minutes before and began marking rows, wishing her mother hadn't caught her dancing. Not that Catriona would mind—she might even understand a little. But Echo did not expect, or even wish, to be understood. She understood herself, so she did not need other people to understand her.

Catriona was only slightly taller than her daughter, dressed in the same simple homespun. Her light brown hair was loosely arranged on top of her head, and her calm grey eyes gave no sign that she had noticed anything out of the ordinary. There was about Catriona a quiet strength, a steadiness that made those around her feel more peaceful without ever a word being said.

Echo marked to the end of the field and then picked up her hoe and walked back to where her mother was sorting through the seeds, and Phoebe, Catriona's younger daughter, was scratching lines in the dirt with a stick. Echo shot her little sister a look of sympathy. Waiting to be given something to do while the grownups planned out the work was the hardest. She remembered those days all too well herself.

Now however, Echo crouched beside her mother and looked over the small parcels of seed laid out on the ground. There were round, brown cabbage seeds, kohlrabi that looked almost the same, the tiny specks that were lettuce, the tinier ones that were spinach, and wrinkled and dried peas and beans. The moon was waxing now, almost full, and it was the time to plant leafy crops that grew above the ground. Next week, when the moon began to wane, they would plant turnips, parsnips, carrots, onions, and other crops that grew below the ground.

"I think we should plant a few rows of beans at the edge of the field first," said Catriona, "then the greens. That way the spinach and lettuce will be more sheltered."

"Yes," agreed Echo, "then we could do peas on the other side, and what if we left room in between for the radishes and stuff as well?"

Catriona looked thoughtfully from the field to the seeds and back again. "That would be best," she said. "We could even alternate so we have beans or peas, then the more fragile stuff, then beans again, and so forth. Now how much spinach do you think we should plant..."

By the time Catriona and Echo had a plan, the sun was a little higher in the sky and Phoebe had drawn an elaborate design on the ground with her stick.

Catriona began dropping bean seeds in the first row Echo had marked, spacing them carefully. Echo called Phoebe over and showed her how to cover the seeds. "The beans get about so much dirt, see?" Echo demonstrated. "Now you try."

Phoebe brushed dirt into the row, covering the seeds. "Like that?"

"Yes, and remember the greens get much less. You will take a handful of dirt and just sprinkle it on—like this—because the greens still need light to grow."

"I remember," said Phoebe.

"Good, and then to pack the dirt around the seeds you can step on it like this—" Echo stood up and stepped carefully along the row, placing her feet one right in front of the other so that every inch of the row was packed down. She turned back and smiled at Phoebe. "Now you try it."

Phoebe stepped carefully along the row they had just covered.

"Good!" approved Echo. "You are lighter than me, too, so that should be just about right. I had better mark the next row before mother finishes this one—" glancing at their mother already about halfway down the field— "so do you think you can manage this now?"

Phoebe nodded, already brushing dirt over the next section, so Echo picked up her hoe again and began marking out the next row, and the three of them settled into a routine for the morning. Echo worked carefully, pulling the hoe in short, precise strokes through the dark earth. She made the rows as straight as possible, using a tree as a guide, and was careful not to make them either too deep or too shallow. She tried to stay a few rows ahead of her mother. From time to time, she would catch a glimpse of neighbors in the fields around them planting as well.

The sun climbed higher and higher in the sky. Sweat trickled down Echo's neck. Her back ached from stooping over the long rows. Her hands, softened over the winter, had red marks from the rough wood of the hoe handle. There would likely be a blister tomorrow. But the long rows stretched out behind them, planted with the seeds that would mean food for winter. And the day was so beautiful that it was worth being alive, Echo thought, just to be outside on a day like this.

She let her mind wander as she worked. As long as the task was fairly simple, she had found she could give part of her attention to what she was doing and daydream as much as she liked. Thinking was easier, anyway, when the hands were busy. She dreamed up a new story and forgot her hands and back, although she did not cease to be aware of the beauty of the day.

She had started by thinking about seeds. Tiny, dried out, and shriveled, it was incredible that they should grow into green and beautiful plants. And not just the garden seeds. An acorn small enough to fit in her hand could grow into the most towering, enduring tree of them all. Echo's mind drifted on, as it usually did, to stories. An idea had sprung into her head about the life of an oak tree. Not just the tree of course, but the people, the people who planted it, watched it grow, and lived under its shelter. There would be generations of them, their fate twined with that of the tree itself... Echo could see the story clearly in her mind, much more clearly, in fact, than she saw the row she was marking or the trees that lined the small field. She never found even the most tedious work monotonous, because there was always a chance to think, and her thoughts were always interesting, at least to herself.

The sun climbed towards its zenith as the long hours slipped past, until at last it was time to stop for lunch. Echo finished the row she was marking and then leaned her hoe against a tree as she joined her mother and sister at the edge of the field.

"A good morning's work," said Catriona, looking over the long, neat rows. She brushed some loosened strands of hair out of her face with the back of her hand. The back was cleaner than the front, but even so, it left a streak of dirt on her forehead. "By next week, we should finish with the first planting."

Echo pushed her own hair back, making a mental calculation of the work done, and the work still left to do. "We've made a good start," she agreed.

She took one of Phoebe's hands and swung it gently. "Tired, little sister?" she asked.

"I'm hungry," said Phoebe. "How quickly will this food grow?"

Catriona laughed and took Phoebe's other hand. "Not quickly enough for lunch!" she said. "Let's go back to the house and get something to eat."

The three of them walked back to the village, stopping at the well in the center. A cluster of women were already there, washing up in the broad trough filled for that purpose, laughing, chattering, comparing notes on the morning's work. Catriona became one of the group immediately, laughing and talking with them, while Phoebe joined the other children who were splashing happily in the spillway from the trough. A long conduit of fired clay, of ancient and unknown workmanship, it eventually deposited the excess water outside the village. Echo stood among them, but not one of them. She patiently waited her turn at the trough, making no attempt to join in the conversation. The noise and babble rose and fell around her almost without her hearing it—she was vaguely aware of it, but it did not matter. The chatter reached her ears without reaching her mind, disconnected sentences, scraps of conversation.

"...and then she said, 'I told you...'" "Last year, we almost ran out of carrot seeds. They are so finicky, and I don't think I'll have enough for a second planting..." "The sweetest child you ever saw, she never once complained..." "...tripped and fell flat on her face..." "Once in a while I don't mind, of course..."

Echo noticed none of it. She had her head in the clouds, or rather in some distant place of her own making. She was still lost in the joy of creation, adding things to her story, almost watching it grow.

She reached the trough, managing to navigate the crowd successfully, wash her hands and arms efficiently, and respond to a few greetings as if she were thinking of nothing else without giving these things more than a modicum of her attention. Then she fell into step with her mother and sister as they went back to their cottage for lunch.

While eating the meal of bread and fish, Echo left her story for a time to respond to Phoebe's lighthearted chatter and help her mother plan the afternoon's work. They continued the discussion of what should be planted where, and how much of each thing. Echo was careful not to let her mind drift away. Her family would be more noticing than the neighbors if she wasn't paying attention.

After lunch was eaten, and the dishes washed and put away, Catriona and her daughters returned to the field and continued planting. The sun was warmer now, warm enough to make going barefoot and without a cloak quite comfortable. The work seemed harder and the hours longer after the brief rest. Afternoons were somehow always longer than mornings, but this one gradually wore away as the shadows grew longer, and the air grew warmer and then colder again. It was a good day's work, and Catriona, Echo, and Phoebe went home tired but satisfied.

While her mother set about preparing supper, Echo took a bucket from a peg and went out to do the milking. She found Daisy, the cow, waiting patiently by the small pen where her calf was kept. She tied Daisy to the fence and gave the cow a handful of grain to eat while she milked. When the bucket was full, she turned the cow into the little pen to let the calf have its share.

Taking the bucket back to the cottage, she strained the milk and carried it down to the cool, dim cellar. She descended the short flight of steps, leaving the trap door in the cottage floor open so that she could see her way. The familiar, earthy smell of the cellar, mingled with that of stored food and herbs greeted her. Setting the milk on a shelf, she covered it, noting again that the cellar was almost empty. It was a good thing that spring was here. Echo hurried back up the steps, closed the trap door, and went outside through the open cottage door. She stood for a moment, looking at the sky. Then she ran down to the shore in the evening light.

The wind whipped at her hair and clothes as she waited for the boats to come in. They had gone out with the tide this morning, a morning that had promised excellent fishing weather. Now, they came in with the tide, the sails white against the dark water. Her father, brother, and grandfather had all gone out to sea today, for the fish that were the village's main source of trade and brought in what little money anyone had. At this time of year, it was rare for all of them to be gone at once. Spring was the busiest time on the farm, with plowing to be done and grain to be sowed, sheep to shear and a thousand and one other things to do after the long winter. But days like today were rare enough that the men had seized the opportunity of a good catch, and with the vegetable garden, at least, plowed and ready, Echo and her mother and sister had taken over the planting of it.

Echo loved watching the boats come in. She loved the sea, as only one born within the sound of its waves can do, loved it for its beauty and its harshness in every mood and kind of weather. She loved, too, the fierce struggle against the waves and wind, something in her reveling in the age-old battle of man against the elements. And when the boats came in, there was something magical about the white sails of the fleet returning home, safe for another day.

She could see, as the boats drew closer to the shore, that they were riding low in the water. It had been a good day then, a promise fulfilled. Catching sight of her father and Ralph in one of the larger boats, she waved to them. Ralph caught her eye and smiled briefly, but did not take his hand from the tiller to wave back. He was the middle child, between Echo and Phoebe, and although only twelve, already did a man's work in the boats. With his shock of brown hair, serious face, and steady gaze, he was very like his father, both in appearance and in character.

Echo scanned the other boats, spying her grandfather manning his own small craft. It was characteristic of him that he had continued to do this in spite of the fact that any of his family would have seen to it that he never wanted for anything. But then, being independent was a trait that most of the villagers had in common. Her grandfather stood straight, now, hand on the tiller, as upright and indestructible as ever.

Owen had been a daring, adventurous man, laughing often, even, or perhaps especially, when there was little to laugh at. He cared little what anyone might think of him or his doings. A fisherman and farmer like his father before him, Owen had lived in the tiny village of Pebblestone all his life, as had his ancestors for uncounted generations. That did not mean he liked it. As soon as he was old enough, Owen left to see the world, disappearing from the villagers' ken for many years.

He had left his village in spite of gloomy forebodings that he would never come back. He had never intended to come back. But after many years, after trials and hardships and triumphs, after falling in love and winning his bride, after traveling with her to the end of the world and back again, Owen had thought of the village by the sea where he had been born. And for the first time, he thought of it as home. He had returned to Pebblestone, bringing with him his wife and their two small children, and there they had stayed. Three more children were born to Owen and Raya after they came to the village. Owen returned to fishing and farming, and this time he was content. He made a home for himself and his family, and they were happy.

To Raya, coming to the village marked the beginning of the most untroubled, and perhaps the happiest, years of her life. The years of adventure with Owen had been wonderful, but this was a place to put down roots, to live out her life, to raise her children. For her it was a homecoming, despite the fact that she had never seen the village before.

She was a serene and joyous woman, who laughed often and smiled oftener, but had a core of seriousness and strength. Life in the village was rarely easy, but Raya was never heard to complain, and she endured the hardships with as much grace as anyone born there. She never spoke of where she came from, or what her life had been before she married Owen. The villagers questioned her as little as they did him. Even if some were curious, no one cared to risk Owen's anger, for he was accounted a dangerous man when crossed, and he didn't appreciate any prying into his affairs. Aside from this, the villagers' own pride would have kept them from asking questions where none were wanted. With few exceptions, they possessed that too rare talent of minding their own business, and each was usually interested enough in his own affairs to bother too much about his neighbor's unless invited.

Owen was absorbed back into village life as if he had never been away, and, in spite of a slight accent and a somewhat foreign manner, Raya became as much a part of Pebblestone as her husband. In time, people forgot that she had not always been one of them.

Of Owen's and Raya's five children, two were as adventurous and impatient as their father. They, like him, left home when they were young. And although they returned occasionally for brief visits, bringing fantastic gifts and even more fantastic stories, neither had returned for good.

The other three children had stayed in the village, and, in time, raised families of their own. Mark, Echo's father, was one of these. He loved his own part of the land and sea too much to think of leaving it for the rest of the world. What could he find out there that was better than a glimpse of the sea at sunset, sailing home in the evening with a good catch, than the dark earth turning under his plow? To Mark's thinking, life anywhere else could not be better than here.

He married a girl of the village who loved Pebblestone and the life there as much as he did, pretty, warmhearted Catriona. Echo was their first child, followed by Ralph, and then Phoebe.

Phoebe was a sweet, sunny-haired child, who brought life and joy to all around her. She sang from morning till night as she gathered shells on the shore or nuts from the woods. She asked innumerable questions, endlessly curious about the world. People who heard her laugh could not help smiling themselves.

Ralph was very like his father, already hard-working and serious though he was still a boy. He loved the sea even more than the farm, spending time in the fishing boats from the time he was a small child. He was already quite a competent fisherman, going out with his father every day and sometimes taking the boat out himself when Mark needed to tend to the farm.

Echo was a teller of stories. As a child, she would listen

in fascination to any tale her grandfather could tell. Her mother, too, knew all the stories told in the village and would tell these to Echo and the other children while she worked. Echo learned other stories from the travelers that occasionally passed through the village, listening and remembering every word. Having once heard a story, she could then retell it, and she possessed a knack for this as well. She always found the right words, the right expression and tone of voice, to capture her audience and make a story live. She knew so many stories that almost any conversation, any happening could remind her of one. Often she would say, "I know a story about that," or "something like that happens in a story I know." Her brother and sister sometimes teased her about this. To Echo, stories and life were tangled together, each leading to the other, and she could not imagine life without stories. Her whole way of looking at things, her whole way of seeing the world, had been formed by the stories that had become a part of her.

Pushing her windswept hair out of her face, Echo waved to her grandfather. Her hair was loose, as usual, blowing out around her in a soft, black cloud. It got in the way, sometimes, but she would rather have it that way than tied up. The sand was warm from the sun and damp from the sea, and she wiggled her bare toes in it. She also disliked wearing shoes and never did when she could possibly avoid it.

The boats touched the sand, and the men leaped out to haul them up onto the shore. Echo perched on a post out of the way to watch. The breeze died down, and the air held the stillness of evening. She watched the sea and the sky. They provided an odd contrast today. The clouds were stretched in an irregular pattern across the sky, some fat and fluffy, others long and thin, some grey, some white, some touched with color by the sinking sun. The clouds never moved, hanging as motionless as if they had been painted across the blue bowl of the sky. The water, on the other hand, was ceaselessly moving, waves rising and falling, washing up onto the sand and running back into the sea. Rolling continually toward the shore and back out again, the noise of them constant and ever-changing. Echo never tired of watching the sea or the sky. She loved the sky always, when it was clear blue, when white clouds blew across it, when they hung still and lazy in the heat of summer. When sunrise and sunset streaked it with color, when clouds hung grey and heavy, when rain stretched a bow across it. She loved the sea too, stormy or calm, in all of its moods. The sea and the sky seemed sometimes to reflect each other, one mimicking the other. On other days, as today, they were stubborn opposites, ignoring each other, each going its own way.

Echo had lived her whole life beside the sea, but she never grew tired of looking at it. *Trying to fill your eyes with the sea is like trying to fill your mind with eternity*, she thought, as she looked at it now. *One is as impossible as the other.*

The men worked quickly, unloading the boats, cleaning the fish and salting it away. Knives flashed and flew, barrels were filled and carted away, the smell of fresh fish was strong in the air. The men shouted back and forth, talking and laughing as they worked, pleased with the catch. Before the last of the light had disappeared from the sky, the fish had been stored and the boats sluiced with water and drawn high enough up the beach to be out of reach of the tide. Echo left before they had finished, stopping at her father's boat on the way.

"Hello, father, hello, Ralph," she greeted them. Ralph was swilling a last bucket of water around the bottom of the boat, while his father tightened the lid on a barrel of fish.

"Hello, Echo," Mark said. Ralph merely nodded. "I left some fish out for supper. How did the planting go?"

Echo picked up the fish and looked around for something to carry them in. Ralph quietly handed her the leather bag that had held his and his father's lunch that morning. "Thank you," she told him as she started filling the bag. "Pretty good," she answered her father. "Another day, and we will finish up the greens and Cole crops, I think."

"That's good," Mark said. "Ralph and I will likely be fishing again tomorrow, as long as you all can keep managing by yourselves."

"I don't see why we couldn't," said Echo cheerfully. She swung the bag of fish. "I had better go start cooking these if they are to be ready in time for supper. You remember that grandfather and grandmother are coming?"

"I remember."

Echo walked quickly back toward the village, calling out, "See you at supper!" as she passed her grandfather's boat. The sun had almost set, though the twilight would last a little longer.

At the cottage, she took out a pan and fried the fish over the fire. Her mother had cooked some of the few remaining vegetables from last year's stores and made a fresh batch of bread. Phoebe set the table and set out the fresh bread to go with the meal. Echo eyed the food critically and decided that she would make soup out of all the leftovers tomorrow. She could use some of the milk to make a white broth. It would be a nice change.

There was a knock at the open cottage door, and Echo ran to welcome her grandmother. Catriona stepped forward. "Come sit down," she invited, smiling. "The boys should be here in a minute." Catriona sat down as well, and she and Raya discussed the weather, a much more important topic to farmers and fishermen than to ordinary people.

Echo flew about, putting the finishing touches on the supper. The men came in shortly afterwards, and there was a clatter of chairs as everyone found a seat around the long, wooden table. There was a hush as Mark asked a blessing, and then a renewed clatter as people helped themselves to food and handed dishes around the table. No one spoke much, except for an occasional request for something to be passed, until the plates were at least half empty. It had been a long day, and everyone was hungry.

Raya was the first to break the silence. "How long do you think this fishing spell will last?" she asked.

Owen considered. "Three days, maybe a week," he said finally. "What do you think Mark?"

Mark put in his opinion, and they all laughed and chattered, telling each other what had happened during the day, happy in a good day's work, a good meal, and the springtime.

Echo looked around the table. At her father, glad of the promise of a good year. At her mother, smiling and content, adding a word to the conversation here and there. Catriona loved this time of day, Echo knew, when the work was done and she had her family around her, relaxed and happy. At her grandmother, poised and serene, beautiful still with her pure white hair and her dark eyes. Echo wondered what she was thinking. One could never tell with Raya. At her grandfather, keen-eyed and direct, saying what he wanted clearly, without wasting words. *And what did he think about?* wondered Echo. *His years of adventure? The fishing? What was needed to keep the boat seaworthy?* Ralph was eating quietly, sometimes adding to the chronicle of the day's fishing. He flushed with pride when his father praised his handling of the boat. Phoebe chattered intermittently, laughing and making those around her laugh at her recital of the day's doings.

After eating, and a leisurely clearing up, the family drifted outside. A fire had been built in the village square, and the villagers were gathering around it. Echo sat with her back to the flames, the light flickering over her hair and casting shadows on her face. She was the storyteller, and it was time for a story. The villagers gathered around in a half circle to listen.

There was an expectant hush, and Echo spoke. "Once upon a time," she began, using those magic words that every story begins with, whether someone says them or not.

The story she told was one she had always liked, the tale of a fisherman who loved his bride so much that he journeyed to the vastness of the sky and stole a single star out of the night for her. It was not one that she had made up—she never told those—but one she had heard years ago from a traveling trader. Her words filled the darkness, and she made the story come alive with the rise and fall of her low, clear voice, the expression of her mobile face, the movement of her slender hands. She could *see* the story as she told it, and she made the villagers see it too. The fire crackled and burned as Echo spun out the tale, sending sparks toward the sky to join the countless thousands of stars.

She came to the end and stopped, her last words still hanging in the air. It was a moment of magic, this, before the wonder of the story left, and everyone returned to earth and everyday. Standing up in the silence, she slipped away from the firelight into the darkness as the rest of the villagers began to drift away or gather in groups to chat. Echo never liked to have to talk to anyone after telling a story. For a while, she lived in another world, and it took her longer than the listeners to come back to earth.

Finding herself on the fringe of a group of girls, she listened with one ear to their laughter and chatter. She had never had any close friends her own age, and she was honest enough to admit that it was entirely her own fault. She had never seemed to get into the habit of talking to them or been interested in the things they talked about. However, the grandmothers and grandfathers of the village were always happy to see Echo. She talked easily with them and was always willing to listen endlessly to their stories.

The night air was chilly, and she shivered, wondering if it was worthwhile to go back to the cottage for her cloak. Her parents would probably be talking for a while, and unless she moved back closer to the fire, she was going to get pretty cold. But she didn't feel like going back just yet. Instead, she sat down on a stone that edged someone's garden and wrapped her arms around her knees. She stared up into the sky and dreamed.

She was looking at the sky, not really seeing it, when suddenly everything seemed to shiver, and she was jerked into awareness. Others had noticed as well, and there was a sudden hush as the villagers stopped talking and looked up.

Watching with a tight, unbelieving feeling in her stomach, Echo saw the sky shiver again, and the moon move, not slowly with its usual imperceptible orbit, but quickly, impossibly quickly, streaking downwards towards the earth. It screamed across the sky, fire trailing behind it, and she saw it disappear over the horizon. She saw, but she didn't believe. It seemed unreal. It *was* unreal. Impossible.

A second after it disappeared over the horizon, the ground shook with the impact of the moon hitting the earth. A shiver went through the earth, as a moment before one had gone through the sky, then everything was still. The hush in the village lasted a moment longer, as the people tried to understand that the incomprehensible had just happened. Then, everyone began talking at once, voices rising to a clamor, fearful, disturbed, apprehensive, questioning, exclaiming, doubting. Questions that had no answers, cries that had no response, fears that could not be dispelled.

Echo felt tired and cold. She got dizzily to her feet and stumbled toward where she had last seen her family. As she did so, she heard her father's voice cut through the clamor. What had happened was a disaster, he said, the consequences of which were not yet known, but nothing could be done about it now. The best thing to do, he told them, was to go home and wait for morning. Getting into a panic now would not help anything.

His voice was steady and reassuring, and the people were steadied and reassured. There was a general murmur of agreement, and the villagers began returning to their homes. As the crowd thinned, Echo reached her family. Ralph took her hand, and she held his tightly, not sure who was comforting whom. "But it's the *moon*," Echo heard her mother say. "It can't just fall out of the sky."

"It can't," said Owen grimly. "But it did."

Chapter Two

Half awake, Echo rubbed the sleep out of her eyes and pushed back her blankets. It was early morning, and the quiet, even breathing from the other bed told her that Phoebe was still asleep. There was a tight feeling in the pit of her stomach, a sense of apprehension. She remembered the moon, and the apprehension deepened to dread.

The loft room where she slept was still mostly dark, the gray light of early morning filtering dimly through the single window. It smelt sweetly of straw from the thatched roof that sloped low overhead. The room was half the size of the cottage, as the loft was divided into two parts with Ralph's room on the other side of the thin wooden wall.

Echo slipped out of bed and into her clothes. She tiptoed out of the room, careful not to wake her sister, and scrambled quietly down the ladder into the main room of the cottage. She opened the door and stepped outside.

The world had that lovely stillness that it does in the most beautiful of early mornings. The eastern sky was streaked with orange and gold, the flaming sphere of the sun just visible over the horizon. The birds were all singing as if disaster could never come. In the pasture, Daisy mooed complainingly, waiting to be milked. Echo breathed deeply. At least the world had not entirely ceased to function.

Mark was stirring up the fire when she went back inside, and Ralph and Phoebe were setting the table while Catriona prepared breakfast. Echo went to help her mother. Mark looked up from the fireplace. "How was it?" he asked.

"Things appeared surprisingly ordinary," Echo told her father as she stirred the pancake batter.

"The moon can't just fall out of the sky without consequences." Catriona's usually cheerful face was troubled. She could take hunger or sickness or the longest, coldest winter without complaining. These were things that she knew how to fix or how to bear, and Echo had seen her make everyone's burden lighter through the most difficult times. But no one knew what to do now. Still, Catriona put breakfast together to feed her family and voiced no more of her fears.

Breakfast was a quiet meal, unlike the cheerful chatter at supper the night before. Ralph said very little, and even Phoebe seemed subdued. They ate hastily and then hurried outside. Echo milked the cow while Ralph fed and watered the calf. Then Ralph went down to the shore after his father. Echo turned Daisy in with the calf and carried the milk inside. She strained it and put it in the cellar, washed the breakfast dishes, and turned the cow back out to graze before heading to the garden to find her mother.

Catriona was looking through her seeds. "I'm not sure what to plant," she told Echo, "Or if I should plant anything at all. We have always planted by the moon, and now..." she trailed off and looked helplessly at her daughter.

Echo had no idea what to say. It was true, they had always planted by the moon, depending on it nearly as much as the sun for a timekeeper. "Perhaps we should just keep on with what we were planting yesterday," she suggested finally. "What else can we do?"

"You are right." Catriona pulled herself together. "Echo, why don't start marking rows again. I will put in the rest of the lettuce. Phoebe!" she called, getting the attention of her youngest daughter who was building a miniature wall out of pebbles. "Phoebe, you can cover the seed when I have finished planting. Remember, this is lettuce, so not too much dirt now, just sprinkle it on, that's right..."

They had planted only a few rows, however, when Echo looked up and saw her father and Ralph returning from the shore. Catriona was watching them with a puzzled expression. The boats should have been out to sea by now and were not expected back until evening. There was no sign of a storm that would drive them home early.

Mark went to talk to Catriona, and Ralph came over to Echo. "We waited for the tide," he said, not looking at her. "We were ready to go out with it like we do every morning. But the tide never went out." He looked up, then, his earnest face troubled. "The water hasn't moved."

Echo was quiet, taking in this new information. Like all seagoing people, she lived by the tides, and she fully understood the seriousness of Ralph's news. They depended on the sea. If the tides ceased to exist... "It's because of the moon," she said. "It has to be."

Ralph nodded but said nothing more. There was nothing to say.

* * *

Echo stood on the fringe of a crowd, letting the voices wash over her without really listening. Instead, she was thinking. Not about stories, for once, but about what she was going to do. She had known, really, since she had watched the moon fall out of the sky. Everything that had happened since had only served to strengthen her determination. It was simple, really. The moon had fallen from the sky. So someone had to put it back.

The villagers had gathered in the square to discuss the fall of the moon and its attendant calamities. "We can still fish," Mark was saying. "We just have to calculate without the tides. We will have to do our best and carry on. After all, we are no strangers to hard times."

There was a general murmur of agreement. Of course, this was beyond anything the villagers had ever faced before, but what else could they do?

Echo knew what else she could do. She was going after the moon.

She slipped away from the meeting and went back to the cottage. Finding a rucksack that was sometimes used for carrying vegetables, she began packing. She packed carefully, deciding what to take. Her shoes went on the bottom. They were a good pair, not as worn as they might have been, since she wore them as little as possible. On a long journey, however, she might need them. A change of clothes went next, and she set a water skin to one side. She would need that, but the rucksack was hardly a convenient place to carry it. She set her cloak out, too. The weather was growing warmer, but she could use it as an extra blanket at night. And who knew how long she would be gone? She reached up into the thatch of the roof and took down a small bag holding all of her savings, which she tucked away in a corner of her pack. Money was a useful thing to have when traveling. Next, she packed as much food as she could without making the load too heavy, dried meat, dried fruit, hardtack, salt, and flour, things that would not spoil on the journey. She took a blanket from her bed as well, folding it as small as she could and tucking it into the pack.

Saying goodbye, telling them that she had to go, was difficult. She felt awkward, not knowing what to say. She wished she could just slip away into the mist one morning and not say anything at all. She hated fuss and hated even more to be the center of attention—unless she was telling a story. At least she need not take leave of the villagers at large. They would hear after she left that she had gone—and why. But to her closest family, farewells must be said.

Instinctively, she went to her grandfather first, knowing that he would understand the best. He was shaping a new oar, the long shavings curling away under his knife and dropping into a pile around his feet. He looked up when Echo came into the yard but said nothing. She perched on a nearby block of wood and watched him work for a few minutes. "I'm going after the moon," she said finally.

Another shaving curled to the ground. "Are you?" he asked, raising one eyebrow.

Echo fiddled with a loose thread of her dress. There was nothing to say to that. Her grandfather understood too well. He, too, had left the village, and she was very like him in some ways. Owen knew that she was going, not just to find the moon, but to find the world. He had looked for it himself and had found his world when he found Raya.

Owen looked up and smiled suddenly. She smiled back, relieved.

"Come along, then," he said, "I have something for your

journey."

Echo followed her grandfather into his cottage where Raya was sitting in the light from the window, spinning wool.

"Echo is going to look for the moon," Owen remarked conversationally, rummaging for something in one of the cupboards. "Ah, here it is." He handed a small leather bag to Echo. "Flint and steel. There is a lot of wilderness between here and the moon, and anyway, you never know when you might need to start a fire. Well," he cleared his throat and patted her shoulder, "good luck and watch out for snakes." He went back outside.

Raya stood up, came around to Echo, and hugged her hard. "Wait here a minute," she said, "I have something to give you as well." She disappeared into her room and reappeared a moment later carrying a small object wrapped in cloth. She handed it to Echo without explanation. The object, whatever it was, was surprisingly heavy for its size. Echo folded back the cloth and saw a sort of medallion, made of gold, with a string threaded through a hole on one edge so that it could be worn around the neck. There was a design on one side of the medallion, a bird that Echo did not know surrounded by flames. It was intricately made, the feathers and the fire mingled together, so that it was impossible to tell where the bird ended and the flames began. She looked at it carefully and then looked at her grandmother. "Wear it," said Raya. "There may be a time when you need it."

Echo obediently put the string over her head and tucked the medallion under her dress. She knew better than to appear to carry valuables while traveling, and she knew better than to ask her grandmother for explanations. Raya had said as much as she was going to say, but as Echo walked back to her own cottage, she wondered again about her grandmother's past and what it was that Raya had never spoken of.

When Echo went back into the cottage, she found her family gathered inside. The meeting in the village must be over. She figured it was best not to put things off. "I'm going after the moon," she said.

Catriona was the first to speak. "When?" she asked quietly.

"Tomorrow." Echo shifted her feet. "The way things are, it seems like something should be done soon."

"I had better see if the clothes are dry," said Catriona. "You'll want some extra things to take with you." She went out to where the washing was drying on the line, and Ralph and Phoebe slipped away as well.

Mark looked troubled. "I should go myself," he said. "At least I shouldn't let you go alone."

"You have a family to take care of," Echo pointed out reasonably. "And the village needs you, too. Who knows what will happen before I can bring the moon back?"

Mark knew this as well as she did, so he said nothing more about it. Instead, he rummaged through the shelf that held some of his tools and fishing tackle until he found a sheathed knife. He extended the handle to Echo. "Here. You'll need this in the woods."

Echo drew the knife from the sheath and looked at it, feeling the weight and the fit of the handle to her hand. It was well-made, with good balance and a plain handle. The knife was of the kind that could be used for almost anything, from skinning game to trimming branches, a necessary tool in the wilderness.

Mark rummaged again. "Here," he handed her a whetstone.

"Thank you." Echo scrambled up the ladder to add the knife to her pack. When she came back down again, Catriona was coming in with an armful of clothes. Echo helped her put them away, adding a few things to her pack. Then she went outside. Turning the corner of the cottage, she found Ralph with some snares in his hands.

"I made these," he held them out to her. "Take them with you, you can catch small game, at least, to help with food."

"I'll do that." She turned the snares over in her hands. "These are very good, Ralph."

He looked at her seriously. "Come back soon."

"I will do my best," she said. It was as much as she could promise.

She wandered aimlessly toward the shore and found Phoebe already there, holding a pink conch shell and looking at the sea. Phoebe turned at the sound of her sister's footsteps, the wind tangling her golden hair across her face. "Why do you have to go?" she asked wistfully.

"Someone has to bring the moon back," Echo said. *But I would have gone anyway,* she thought. *I would always have gone. The moon just gives me a reason to go.* Her mind leapt in excitement at the thought of the journey ahead, and she felt the thrill of it in her bones. There was so much to see, so much of the world that she knew only through stories. She felt apprehension, too, and for a moment she was tempted to stay, to not worry about the moon, let everything work itself out, stick to the life she knew. The world was so big, there was so much that could go wrong. But even as she thought it, she knew she would go. There was something in her pulling her outward. She did want so much to see what was on the other side of the forest, what lay beyond the horizon.

Phoebe offered her sister the shell. "I found this for you," she said. "So you can listen to the ocean when you are lonely for us."

Echo scooped her sister up, shell and all, and held her tight. "I am lonely for you already," she said.

Phoebe squirmed. "Put me down! I am too big to be held."

"I know." Echo gave her sister one last squeeze and set her down on the sand.

* * *

She came down very early the next morning, but her mother was already up, setting loaves of fresh-baked bread on the table. Echo hesitated a moment, then went to her, and they hugged each other tightly. After a moment, Catriona drew back. "Every child who is born brings a little magic into the world," she said. "Your magic was so strong, my beautiful girl, my firstborn child. Perhaps that is why you must go, because there is something waiting for you to do. Go with my blessing and my love."

Echo managed to smile a little, though her eyes were wet. "Do not worry for me, Mother," she said. "I am not expecting this to be easy, but it's something that I have to do. And I won't forget who I am or where I come from."

The brilliant color of the sunrise was fading from the sky as she left the village. Catriona had wrapped up a few of the fresh loaves of bread and given them to her before she left. Last goodbyes had been said, last hugs given. "Be careful," Mark had said as she was leaving. "If you get hurt out there in the wilderness, there won't be anyone to help you. You'll be alone. And even more than the moon, we want you to come back."

Now she was on her way, the village invisible behind her as she made her way through the forest. Her heart lifted in excitement. She was going somewhere at last. The world was out there, and she was going to see it. The moon had fallen to the north, so that was the direction that she went, across the field that she had been planting only the day before, and into the trees. There was no road to follow. The forest was unexplored, as far as the villagers knew. As Echo walked on, she saw nothing to contradict this. Before her was wilderness. Behind her, only the track of her own feet.

The excitement didn't really go away, but it soon dimmed under the reality of walking. One foot in front of the other, one step after another, deeper and deeper into the forest. The shade of the trees kept the morning coolness for a long time, but by late afternoon it was hot and airless. She missed the free-blowing wind of the seashore. The scenery didn't change much, but Echo wasn't really bored. The quiet gave her plenty of time to think, or to dream.

She had sometimes wondered what people did who had no recourse to their own thoughts. What would it be like to always have to be busy or entertained, to always need someone nearby for conversation, to never appreciate the silence? Being a storyteller, she could imagine it; being herself, she could not fathom it.

She walked until nightfall. The sunlight slanting through the trees helped her keep her direction, as did the roar of the sea on her left side. She walked toward where she had seen the moon fall. Although she was sure of her direction, she did not know, and had no way of knowing, what lay between her and it.

When it began to grow dark, she stopped to make camp. She had come a long way and was tired. The warmth of the day had disappeared, so she was feeling rather chilled as well. A stream was babbling over some rocks nearby and this seemed like a good place to stop. She would need the water, and perhaps she might catch some fish.

Other than the stream, there was nothing to mark this place from any other she had passed through that day. The woods still looked the same, the same kinds of trees, the same underbrush. It was as good a place as any.

Echo dumped her pack near a maple, glad to be rid of its weight. She stretched, feeling a little less tired. There was plenty of dead wood around, branches that had fallen with the weight of ice and snow last winter, or the one before that, or the one before that. She gathered some of it into a pile, collected a few handfuls of dry dead leaves, broke the smallest twigs off the branches for kindling, and lit a fire.

Once the fire was going, she took her snares and went down to the stream. She set the traps near the water, hoping they might catch animals coming to drink, then moved upstream a little way and managed to catch a few fish. After cleaning the fish, she brought them back to camp where she cooked them over the fire. These, together with the bread her mother had sent, made a good meal.

After she had eaten, Echo cut some leafy branches from the young trees growing nearby. She made a bed of them on the ground near the fire. With her cloak for a pillow, she wrapped herself in her blanket and settled down to sleep.

Awakening in the first grey light of lifting darkness, she listened. A bird was singing, then another took up the chorus, and another and another until the forest was full of music. Not all was light and music, though. The blanket was wet with dew when she pushed it aside and scrambled to her feet. But that was to be expected. She stretched, breathing deeply, taking the cold spring air into her lungs.

Taking her water skin, she walked down to the stream where she washed her face and hands. She emptied the water skin, rinsed it out, and refilled it with fresh water. She checked the snares, but both were empty, so she unset them and took them back to camp with her. Taking some bread out of the pack, she put the traps and the blanket in it. Then she set off again, munching the bread as she went.

The grass, bushes, and other undergrowth of the forest were wet with dew. Every leaf and blade of grass carried its shining load. Echo saw a dozen spiderwebs, each thread coated with moisture, shimmering and beautiful. Her feet were soon wet, and the bottom of her skirt was soaked through from brushing against the leaves as she walked. Eventually, she kilted up her skirt to keep it from slapping wetly against her legs. There was no one to see her anyway.

The sun grew brighter and hotter, and by noon the dew had dried. Echo spread her blanket over the rucksack, tying it there to dry as she walked. She ate some more bread for lunch. It needed to be eaten soon anyway, before it grew moldy or stale. After this, she would cook enough meat each night for supper, and lunch the next day. Not stopping to cook lunch as well as supper would save time.

The days passed, long, lonely, and peaceful, each like the one before. The forest had not changed much, and there was little to separate one day from another. The days grew gradually warmer, and the nights too. Echo was able to find berries as well as greens for her meals. There were still fish, and, less reliably, whatever she could catch in her snares. When the bread ran out, she made more from the flour in her rucksack, mixing it with water from whatever stream she was camped next to. She had the dried meat too, when she needed it.

The pack rubbed her shoulders and weighed her down at first, until she grew so used to it that she hardly noticed it anymore.

Her feet, softened with a winter of wearing shoes, grew hard and calloused again. For the most part, the ground was soft enough for her to go barefoot without trouble. The first few days, her muscles had ached from the unaccustomed amount of walking, but she was stronger now.

And still, the days and miles slipped away, so much behind, and so much still ahead. Sometimes, when the trees grew thicker and the forest blocked out the sun, Echo would climb a tree, high enough that she could see the sky, to be sure of her direction. Going in circles in the woods was all too easy—one moved a little to go around this tree, a little to pass that bush and the direction was lost. She no longer had the ocean for a guide. The land must extend farther here, and the sea was some distance away. Still, she had inherited her grandfather's unerring sense of direction, and that helped her. When she could, she camped for the night in a clearing, hungry for the sight of the sky after walking for days under the trees. She would lie on her back and look up into a night sky that was lit only by stars.

It was only when Echo looked back that she thought the time had passed rather quickly. The days, unbroken by events, seemed to take up little time. They had slid into weeks almost without her being aware of it. And yet, it seemed as if she had been walking through the forest for a lifetime. That morning when she left the village felt distant and far away.

Being this completely alone gave Echo time to think. She had always been alone in a way, and always been thoughtful, but now she found herself seeing things as if from a great distance, perhaps in a slightly different way, more clearly than she had seen them before.

She had never been truly at home in her own village, and she had not even minded, but now she wondered if she had missed something.

She remembered saying once to someone that she had no friends. She had laughed when she said it, but later the memory of her words had made her think; and she had realized that it must be true. If she did have a friend, she would not have been able to say that aloud—or even to herself—without feeling as if she was betraying that person. But she had said it easily, so it was true. She had no friends.

She knew that she had always been an outsider in her own village. Not that she was looked down upon, or that anyone was ever unkind to her. Even if she had been incapable of standing up for herself, Owen, not to mention her own father, would never have allowed that. But she had never had close friendships among the village girls. She had never taken an interest in the things they were interested in, never joined in the chattering, the gossip, the quarrels, the fun. She did not want to add ribbons to her dress or try a new way of fixing her hair or wonder which boy would ask her to dance at the next celebration. She knew most of the villagers by name and would exchange greetings with the other girls when they crossed her path, but they had nothing to talk about. Echo knew that this was her own fault. If she had been more like them, she would have been one of them. But she wasn't. The things that mattered to her were irrelevant to the other girls, and the things that mattered to them were unimportant to her.

She had never looked twice at any of the village boys, either. Not, she admitted in all honesty, that any of them had ever looked twice at her. But this, again, was her own fault. None of the boys wanted a sweetheart whose mind was a million miles away.

The thing was, she did not even mind that much. Not about not having a sweetheart, and not about not having a friend. She supposed if she had minded, she would have made more of an effort to fit in. But she really did not want to. She would rather be herself, different, than like everyone else. She walked her path alone, and although she was sometimes lonely, she never regretted what she was or wished to be different. She knew enough stories to know that there is at least one oddball or uncertain character in every village, and she didn't entirely mind being Pebblestone's. In an odd way, it did give her a place of a sort, although not one she would be content to occupy forever.

She had dreams, of course, rather undefined, but all the more attractive for that, because they were whatever she wanted them to be at that moment. You could count on dreams to change with you, grow as you did. Realities were less certain.

She did not think things would ever change for her, at least not in the village. Echo told her stories to the villagers, and they listened and were proud of her, but as a curiosity or a prodigy, not as one of themselves. There were too many things that set her apart, not the least her way of shutting out the noise as if listening to something unheard by others, her way of looking right through a person with her odd, golden eyes at something beyond. No one likes to be made to feel insignificant, least of all the proud inhabitants of a windswept village. Even if the one making them feel insignificant is unaware of it. Perhaps even more so.

The villagers themselves were too proud, too independent, to be more than mildly affected by Echo. Many of them liked her well enough, and all listened to her stories. But she was the grit in the oyster, the wrench in the works, the thing that didn't fit. She was not just a square peg in a round hole—she was a triangular one. She was not sure that a place could ever be found to fit her, and she was not sure that she would want to fit into it if there was.

During the long, quiet days, there was nothing to do but walk and think. Echo's feet moved automatically, taking her in the right direction, while her mind wandered far away, around the world and to the stars and back again. Sometimes she seemed to have drifted so far away that nothing around her seemed to have any meaning. She was tempted to touch one of the trees, just to see if it was real, but she did not.

Echo did not think too much about the moon in these days, or about what awaited her at the end of her journey. Reaching the moon would only be the beginning. Somehow, she had to find a way to return it to the sky, but she did not let this worry her. She didn't think about whether she was strong or weak, brave or foolish. She simply never thought that there was anything she couldn't do.

For now, there was the journey, the ground under her feet that went on and on, the world that she was seeing at last. For now, that was enough.

And then one morning, when she climbed a tree to be sure of her direction, she saw away to her right a break in the green evenness of the forest. Branches were broken first, the dying leaves pale against the bright green of nearby trees. Then whole trees seemed to be gone, smashed to earth, leaving a large gap in the woods. Echo turned her steps in that direction. She felt a lift of excitement. She had to be close. From the damage to the trees, it looked as if something heavy had fallen on them from out of the sky.

To reach the broken trees was half a morning's walk. When

she was close, Echo had to fight her way through a tangle of branches that were struggling upwards toward the sun from trees that had been knocked down, while scrambling over the trunks of fallen trees. She was hot and breathless when she finally forced her way over, through, and around the mess and came out into an open space.

She could see the scars on the trees where the moon had crashed through. Broken tops and then whole trees knocked over in a slanting downward path as she had seen from the top of a tree half a day's walk away. She had been fighting her way through some of the downed brush for the last half an hour. The moon had fallen here. She could see the furrowed dirt and the crater where it had been. But it was not there now.

Echo scrambled down from the last log and half walked, half slid, into the crater. She looked around, first at the trees, then at the ground. There were wheel tracks there, of a large cart or wagon, cut deeply into the soil as if the wagon had been loaded with something heavy. The tracks were not fresh, but they were not very old, either. A light rain had washed them away in places and blurred the edges, but they were not as old as the last heavy rain, she decided, or they would have washed away completely. She scanned the trees again. Now she could see that away to the east, a path had been cut through them, large enough to admit a wagon. Climbing out of the crater, she followed the tracks.

After walking for another three days, she reached the edge of the trees. The trail must have taken some time, and many men, to cut. It was wide, and clearing roads through this forest was no light task. Echo's apprehension grew as she walked. Someone had gone to a lot of time and effort to take the moon out of the forest, but it was not back in the sky.

Somehow, she had never thought that the moon would not be waiting for her where it had fallen. She saw now that this was silly, that an event like the moon falling would not go unnoticed by the rest of the world, that there must be many villages nearer to the moon than her own.

By the afternoon of the third day, the trees were not so thick. Instead of weeds and undergrowth, grass grew under them, enough light slanting between the branches for it to be thick and green. The whole wood took on a park-like aspect. Echo enjoyed the sunshine and the change from fighting her way through underbrush. The forest had come to an end.

The girl who walked out of it was not quite the same as the one who had walked into it two months before. She was a little thinner, a little browner. She was older too, not just in body, but in mind and soul. No one can spend two months entirely alone without being changed, at least a little. With no one to talk to, there is endless time to think, and that without outside distractions. This can be the making or the breaking of a person. Then, too, there was the knowledge that she was entirely alone, that if she needed help, there would be no one to ask for it, that she must manage by herself, because there was no one else. No one would be there to help her up if she fell. If she became sick or hurt, there would be no one to take care of her, and somehow she would have to feed herself in spite of everything. She had been completely responsible, bearing the entire weight of her own mistakes, where there was no room for mistakes.

The trees became fewer and farther between until Echo was walking between fields. Wide spreading fields, some planted with crops, she noticed, some containing sheep and cattle. The fields were dotted with cottages here and there, and she could see farmers at work tending their crops. The fields and farms and cottages occupied a wide valley that stretched out before Echo like a shallow, elongated bowl. A river twisted along the bottom, and roads wound between the fields and cottages. Interspersing the open spaces were trees, some of them fruit trees that had been planted, Echo decided, some remnants of the forest that must have once filled the valley as well. She could see that across the valley the forest began again, the trees thick and dark once more.

On the other side of the valley, where the river swung closer to the forest, was a high point. The ground sloped away on all sides here, to the river, and back to the trees. The incline was too gradual for it to be called a hill; it was more of a rise in the ground. A city was set on this high point, overlooking the valley, as if protecting it or guarding it. The city was wide, reaching across the river on one side, almost to the forest on the other. The stone of its walls was grey and ancient looking. Echo thought that it must have been there for a long time. It almost looked like part of the surrounding land, as if it had grown there instead of being built.

She had never seen a walled city before, although she had heard her grandfather describe them. Their own village was too poor and too remote to have ever needed to worry about building walls against serious attackers. Then too, there were the boats and the sea, or the forest. If a force too large to fight ever came, the villagers could disappear for a time, harrying their enemies from hiding, returning when the intruders left. They belonged to that bit of earth, to that part of the sea. They could rebuild.

The cart tracks that Echo had been following had joined one of the roads. Looking ahead, across the valley, she could see that it eventually led to the city, which also seemed to be the most likely place to look for the moon. Echo doubted that one of the farmers she could see working in the fields had taken the trouble of cutting a road through the forest for the satisfaction of hiding the moon in his barn. Whoever had taken the moon was someone with power, and with time and money to spare. The city looked like power.

The sight of the people below, the thought of talking to anyone, left Echo with a tight feeling of nervousness. She had not seen or spoken to another human being in a long time. She felt tempted to try saying something out loud, while there was no one else to hear her, just to see if her voice was still working. And these were strangers, people she did not know. In Pebblestone, she knew most of the people by name and their family history to boot. Even when strangers came to the village, she was surrounded by people she did know, a protecting wall of family and neighbors. Now she was alone.

She decided to wait until morning to enter the city. There was no sense in going in now, when it would soon be dark. No, she would go when she had the whole day ahead of her to try to find the moon. Even while thinking this through, she had not stopped walking. By this time, she was about halfway down the valley, and dusk had fallen. She picked out one of the lonelier farms, one with some outlying fields containing haystacks. Having been sleeping outside for two months now, she preferred to continue to do so rather than ask for shelter. Leaving the road, she climbed a few walls and reached the field.

The camping spot she picked was near one of the haystacks, one that was hidden from view by other haystacks and would not be visible from any of the nearby farmhouses. She set her pack on the ground and leaned back into the sweet-smelling hay with a sigh. Rather than risk a fire so close to civilization, she ate some of the dried meat, and bread that was left over from what she had baked two days ago. There was still water in her water skin from the last stream she had passed, as well. When she finished eating, Echo wrapped her blanket and cloak around her, burrowed into the haystack a little, and slept.

* * *

Finding the moon was quite easy after all.

She awoke before first light the next morning, as she had been in the habit of doing since her journey began. Awake, she lay still for a moment, listening, taking stock of her surroundings before even opening her eyes. Birds were singing, a cock crowed on the farm nearby, and farther away, the farmer was calling to his cows. She opened her eyes and saw the hay around her and above that, a sky clear of clouds. The sky was still dark, but blue-gray rather than black, and to the east it was a paler gray touched with orange, where the sun would be rising soon.

She scrambled out of the hay and stood up, stretching, and breathing deeply. She brushed the hay off herself, picking several pieces out of her hair. She shoved her blanket and cloak into her pack. Then, wasting no time, she started toward the road, munching a piece of bread as she went.

At the edge of the road, she stopped. The thick grass of the hayfield was wet with dew, and walking through it had left her feet quite clean. She suspected that it would be wise to wear shoes in the city, and it made sense to put them on now, before her feet became dusty again from the road. Digging in her pack for the shoes, she dried her feet on the edge of the cloak and put them on. This done, she started off again, down the road.

It was early summer, and the morning air was still cool,

though the clear sky promised a hot, cloudless day to come. The dew had partially settled the dust, but where Echo stepped, she left dry footprints on the road. The air held that peaceful, expectant stillness that can only be found on an early summer morning.

As she walked, the farms around Echo began to bustle with life. Roosters crowed, first from one farm, then another, as if to see who could crow the loudest. There was the creak and slam of doors, the impatient bawling of hungry calves, and the more impatient lowing of their mothers, occasionally interspersed with a soothing moo to their offspring. Families talked, or laughed, or called instructions as they did their chores, the words inaudible at this distance, but the voices carrying in the clear air.

A cart piled high with produce rumbled past Echo, and another turned onto the road ahead of her. She had reached the bottom of the valley now, and she crossed the wide, arched bridge over the river. It was made of stone, perhaps as old as the city. She paused near the middle and looked over one balustrade at the river far below. The bridge was made high, she guessed, to allow boats to pass under. It had looked small from the rim of the valley, but standing here it was enormous, wide enough for several carts to pass, and very long. The balustrade was wide too, wide enough to easily walk on if one had wanted to, and high enough that she had to stand on tiptoe to see over.

Once across the bridge, the road began to climb again, upward to the city. The closer she came to the city, the more traffic was on the road. There were carts and carriages, sheep and cattle being driven to market, women with large baskets on their arms, men carrying packs on their backs and staffs in their hands. Chickens squawked complainingly from crates, and children darted around the other travelers while mothers anxiously called them back.

Echo was one of the crowd, unnoticed in the multitude. No one looked her way, and she was glad of it. She wished herself back in the forest, but at least she hadn't had to talk to anyone.

The procession reached the city just before the sun rose. The carts rumbled to a stop, the drivers letting the reins slacken, patiently waiting. Some of the pedestrians gathered in groups, exchanging gossip and news, some stood apart, just waiting. Sheep and cattle milled around.

Having started early, Echo was near the front, and now she wriggled through the last few people to see why everyone had stopped. When she was clear of the crowd she stopped as well, as suddenly as if she had run into a wall, although the closed gates of the city were still fifty paces away.

Chapter Three

They were waiting for the gates to open. That was why everyone else had stopped. Echo realized this dimly in the back of her mind. But that was not why she had stopped. She stood still, staring, not at the closed gates, but at the device emblazoned upon them. The noise of the crowd seemed very far away. Suddenly, she was back in Raya's cottage, looking down at something in her hand, hearing her grandmother's voice saying, "There may come a time when you need this." A medallion, bearing the image of a bird surrounded by flame. And then she was back, standing in the dusty road surrounded by people, staring at the closed gates of a strange city, gates that bore the same image.

The sun crested the horizon, lighting the world, turning grey half-shadows into light and color. Its rays touched the symbol on the gate, changing the wood to flaming gold, and for one moment, the bird seemed alive, dancing in the flames...

A fluttering noise drew Echo's eyes upward. She looked, and saw a flag, emblazoned with the same symbol of the fiery bird, flying from one of the towers that guarded the gate. Her fingers moved to her neck, touching the hard metal of the medallion through the cloth of her dress, wondering what it all meant.

A horn sounded from within the city, a long, clear note. There was the sound of bars being lifted and bolts being pulled back, and then the gates slowly swung open and the traffic began to move. Echo moved with them, taking note of her surroundings as she went. She did not know now why her grandmother had given her the symbol of this city, but if she was meant to know, she would find out in time. Meanwhile, she had come here to find the moon, and she needed to pay attention.

The walls were very thick and high, Echo saw as she walked through the gate. They towered above her, four men high, and wide enough for three to walk abreast. The gates were thick too, made of wood and as high as the walls. A watchtower stood on either side of the gates and at intervals along the wall. Farther away, Echo could see the turrets of a castle, rising above the roofs of the rest of the city.

The city was indeed very ancient, she decided. Sharp edges of stone had been worn smooth by time and use. Streets had been worn down by the passing of many years and many feet until they had sunk into the ground. The place had a feeling of having stood for a thousand years, of having stood for so long on this patch of earth as to have become a part of it, part of the very hills, of the earth itself.

There must have been thousands of stories told in this place, Echo thought. And thousands more that were lived, and are, every day, but never spoken. She brushed her hand over a stone, as if she could absorb the history of it from a touch. As if she could understand this city, and why she, herself, was even now wearing its seal around her neck.

Marketgoers exchanged news with their friends at the tops of their voices. Vendors cried their wares, each trying to be the loudest so as to sell the most. Shoppers and sellers bargained over goods, cheerfully insulting each other and the materials in question with complete good humor and lack of animosity. The scent of fresh baked bread and roasting meat mingled with that of the animals being driven to market and the less pleasant ones of the city and too many people packed together.

Echo found the noise and the bustle overwhelming. She was used to being able to look in three directions without seeing any people, just sky or forest, fields or sea. And for the last two months, she had seen nobody at all. As for the noise... *I thought a dozen women at the well were loud*, she thought. Fighting her way out of the main body of the crowd, she found a quieter area. A woman selling herbs was nearby, but she did not seem to be doing a very brisk business.

Now that she was out of the crowd, an onlooker, not part of it, Echo was able to get her bearings. She leaned back against a wall, glad of the solid, comforting stone. At least she could be sure that there was no one behind her now. The confusion in the marketplace was beginning to make more sense. Everyone was there for something, and went about getting it, or trying to get it, purposefully or dawdlingly according to time and temperament.

"It can be interesting, can't it," said a voice near Echo, "just to look, and also to see, but not to act or do?"

Startled, Echo turned. It was the woman selling herbs who had spoken. She was seated against the wall, with her wares spread out on a brightly colored cloth before her. More bundles were stacked next to her, and she rested one arm on them. At first glance, Echo thought that the woman was quite old, but after a second look, she was not so sure. And the woman's voice had sounded young.

"I came here to do something," said Echo. "Perhaps by watching I can learn how to accomplish it."

"One can learn a lot by watching, but never everything." The herb-woman answered. "But you will not have learned that yet."

"One never knows how much one does not know, because to know what is not known would be a contradiction of terms," said Echo, pleased with both the confusion and the sense of her reply. She could be enigmatical too.

The herb-woman chuckled, honest, good-humored mirth in her laugh. "Well, you'll go your own way, sure enough," she said.

"That's what I'm afraid of," Echo said.

"Never be afraid, child," the old woman answered. "It's not worth it."

"Isn't it?" asked Echo idly. But her mind was not really on what she was saying. She was looking down a side street, where a steady stream of people were coming and going. They seemed quite unrelated to the market-goers, and, indeed, seemed to have nothing to do with the business part of the city. There was rather a holiday air in the passers-by, as if they were sightseers, or tourists.

"Where are they going?" she asked, indicating the side street.

"Ah," the herb woman was serious now. "They are going to see the moon."

"It is in the city, then?" she phrased it as a question, but she already knew the answer.

"That it is. Brought by the king some four weeks back. You can see it for a penny," the woman suggested.

"I believe I will," replied Echo thoughtfully, staring at the ground without seeing it. Then she looked up and smiled at the herb-woman. "Thank you."

The woman's face crinkled again. "It has been a pleasure."

Echo walked steadily toward the side street without looking back. She joined the stream of people, following them along the winding street. Tall houses loomed on either side, shading it from the morning sun. The air between the buildings was close and still. When the sun rose high enough to shine straight down into the street, it would be quite hot.

Echo had walked nearly to the other side of the city before the crowd reached its destination. The streets were a maze, winding here and there with no obvious purpose, sometimes crowded, sometimes close to empty. But she managed not to lose track of the group of sightseers. As they walked, a smaller street opened up into a slightly wider one. She could see the castle to her right, not far away. Directly ahead was an arched entryway, leading into a courtyard. The sightseers were going there, and Echo followed them.

The courtyard was quiet, quiet even with the number of people that were in it. Vines hung the walls, and a few small, city-grown trees lent the place a peaceful, garden-like air. The courtyard was close to the castle, but not quite part of it. It was also close to the edge of the city. So close that the opposite wall of the courtyard was also part of the city wall.

Echo had paid her penny at the entrance, and now she stood just inside the arched entryway. At first, she could see nothing but the trees and the wall and the backs of the people in front of her. She moved forward, worming her way through the crowd, until she stood at the very front and could see what everyone was looking at.

It was the moon, there in the courtyard, resting on a stone pedestal. It shone faintly, even in the daylight. Even though she had expected to see it, Echo felt a shock as she looked at it, the sort of shock one feels when confronted with something impossible. She had seen the moon a thousand times in the sky, but never like this. This was wrong, for the moon to be here, on a stone pedestal, in a city built by men. Something magical and mysterious had been turned into something that people paid a penny to look at. In the sky, the moon was a symbol, a light, a guide. On earth, it was nothing but an unusual piece of rock.

Still, Echo could not tear her eyes away. Even now, it was a sort of symbol, she realized. The moon, here, represented the unreachable within reach, the unattainable attained. Everything that men strive for and never get on display for the world to stare at. It was all wrong, she thought again. Some things weren't meant to be understood.

The low voice of a guard roused Echo at last. "Move along, then," he said, but he said it gently. "Let someone else have a turn to see."

She moved to the edge of the crowd, to a spot near the wall where she could still see the moon. There was a general shift as one group left the courtyard and another came in. She noticed again that the crowd was oddly silent. People looked but said nothing. There was no jostling, no shouting, no commentary. Perhaps there was just nothing to say.

Echo also noticed that the guard who had spoken to her was not the only one. There were several, unobtrusively placed around the courtyard. They were all in uniform, with the seal of the city embroidered on their right sleeves. She looked at the moon again. Now that she was farther away, and more used to it, she wondered if the moon seemed smaller now than it had in the sky. She stared thoughtfully but wasn't sure. After all, distance made it difficult to judge. And it had been a long time since she had seen the moon in the sky.

Leaving the courtyard with the next shift, she thought about what she had to do. She took note of anything that might help her. The courtyard had a wide entrance. Of course, it would have, because they had had to bring the moon into it. As she stepped back into the street, she looked in the opposite direction from that which she had come. The street sloped downward here, ending in a gate set deeply into the city wall. This gate was smaller than the main one by which she had entered the city that morning and would be one of several. She had gathered from stories that cities often had different entrances and exits for different purposes. Echo guessed that nobles used this one when they went hunting. It was close to the castle and would open into the forest. With all the people in front of her, she had not noticed it on the way there.

She turned away and wandered back the way she had come. The houses rose tall on either side, shading the street. She picked up speed, moving briskly, purposefully. She was think- ing, but not about where she was going. She did not see the streets or the buildings around her. Her gaze was turned inward on the wheels turning inside her head.

Somehow, she had to steal the moon. That was what she had set out to do—find the moon and return it to the sky. The only question was how. So she walked as if with purpose, her feet keeping pace with her thoughts, as she considered possibilities and rejected them, considered others and kept pieces of them, until an idea started to take shape.

Somewhere in the back of her mind she knew that she was in over her head. That what she was doing was foolhardy in the last degree. That she was very much alone, and that things could go terribly wrong. But she could not go back to Pebblestone and tell them that she had not tried. Could not see the moon and not make the attempt. Could not give up, now that she had started. She was the stubborn scion of a stubborn race, and she set her mouth and went ahead.

It didn't matter that she was terrified. That her stomach tied itself into knots just thinking about the enormity of the task. That she had no idea what she was doing and had never felt so alone in her life. She pushed all that firmly down. After all, she did not have to think about the whole task, just what needed to be done next. She needed to do what came first, one thing at a time. Like harvesting a field of turnips. It looked enormous when you started, and you wondered how you would ever finish. But it had to be done, so you started pulling turnips, one, and then another. You loaded them into crates and carried them into the cellar, trip after trip until your arms ached and the job seemed interminable. Eventually, you were done. The field was harvested, the turnips stored safely away. Looking back, it did not seem like such a huge task after all.

The sun now beat directly down into the streets. The air was hot and close between the buildings. Echo found herself in the market district, with shops on either side instead of houses. Many of them had awnings in the front, and she moved under these to walk in the shade.

She was still thinking, trying to form the ideas in her head into something workable. No matter how much she thought, she could only see so far ahead. She tried to plan for what might go wrong without considering the possibility of failure. She was used to doing things herself, and she was proud of her self-reliance, but right now she wished she had someone to at least ask advice of. Then she reminded herself that it was no use wanting the impossible, and that she was used to making the best of things.

It was early afternoon when she found herself on a street

near the river with the outline of a plan in her mind. The street was wide here, stretching from the buildings on one side to muddy-looking water on the other. Within the limits of the city walls, the wide but slow-moving river had been tamed into a wider and slower-moving stone lined canal. There was no rail or barrier between the canal and the pavement. The street simply stopped at the water's edge. Iron rings, as old but as lasting as the rest of the city, had been hammered into the stone pavement at intervals for boats to tie at.

There was a great deal of traffic, both on the water and in the street. Echo dodged one group of workmen carrying crates of produce off a boat. Farther on, she skirted around another carrying bales of cloth onto one. Wide, wooden ramps stretching directly from the boats to the street made the process simple and efficient.

Echo continued along the waterfront, scanning the shops and warehouses as she went. She had walked nearly halfway along the River Street before she found what she was looking for. It was a sailmaker's shop, crowded on both sides by tall warehouses, but with much less hustle and bustle going on around it than some of the others. The shop was small, but well-kept, bright and clean with a homey, peaceful air about it.

The door to the shop was propped open, the sunlight streaming in, making an oblong of light on the scrubbed wooden floorboards. A white-haired man sat at a table in the light from one of the windows, stitching at a sail. A boy of about eight, probably the old man's grandson, perched on a stool nearby. He was carving a small boat out of wood, the shavings curling away under his knife and falling into a small pile around his feet. A striped cat was curled up near the edge of a patch of sunshine, dozing peacefully.

Echo stepped inside, waiting for her eyes to adjust to the comparative dimness of the shop after the brightness of the street, and taking in the smell of canvas and wood and tar. There was no scent of salt or brine—that came with the sea, not the river. But for a moment she felt closer to home than at any time since she had left.

The sailmaker looked up when she came in and nodded politely without stopping his work. The little boy, however, stared at her, curious, his work for the moment forgotten.

"Good morning," she said politely, addressing both the sailmaker and his grandson.

"A fine morning to you, miss," the sailmaker returned equably.

"Is that for a lugger?" asked Echo, taking a courteous interest in the sailmaker's work. She stepped further into the shop, taking a closer look at the sail.

"That it is," said the sailmaker approvingly. "You know something about boats, then?"

"My grandfather is a fisherman, and my father, and my brother," she told him. "I grew up around boats."

"Who is your father?" asked the sailmaker. "I know all the rivermen in these parts."

"This is on the sea," said Echo, fingering a piece of canvas. She had been looking around as she spoke.

"A long way from here," said the sailmaker. "We do not have much traffic from the sea. We did, once, but the king discourages it now."

"Why is that?" Echo was interested. She would have thought that more trade would make the city more prosperous.

"It's been that way for years," said the sailmaker vaguely. "Since the old king's time. They say a sailor got the better of him in a disagreement, and he never forgot or forgave."

Echo thought that a very poor reason to ban any kind of sea trade. She also sensed a story, but she didn't ask any more. Instead, she bent down to look at the ship that the boy was carving. It was a cutter, the fine lines evident even in the tiny model. "It's a beautiful ship," she told the child.

"Grandpa says he will help me make a sail for it when I have finished," The boy replied, pleased at her praise.

"Young Nate thinks of nothing but ships and the sea," remarked the sailmaker. "He is determined to be a sailor one day." He spoke half proudly, half sadly.

"A captain," Nate said firmly, whittling industriously at his half-finished boat.

Echo and the sailmaker laughed. "You might as well aim high as aim low," remarked the sailmaker.

"I know a story about a ship," Echo told the boy.

"Did it sail on the sea?" he asked.

"This was a very special ship," she said. "It sailed on air. A flying ship..."

And she told the story, how a young boy, who was a Fool of the World, set out to accomplish an impossible task anyway. To build a flying ship and win the hand of the king's daughter... The Fool of the World had set out on his task in spite of his family's unkindness and discouragement. Through his own kindness and generosity, and the goodness of his heart, the boy had won for himself friends who helped him with his tasks. For even after the boy had delivered the flying ship to the king, the king had demanded another task, and another, reluctant to give his daughter to a poor peasant, even though he had already given his word. But the Fool and his friends had accomplished every task set to them, and the Fool eventually won the hand of the princess, and her love as well.

It was the right story to tell. A story that had nothing at all to do with ships would not have mattered to either of them, and this story was full of humor and adventure, loyal friendship and true love. Both the sailmaker and his grandson were intrigued by the idea of a flying ship.

While Echo spoke, the sailmaker forgot to stitch his sail, and the knife lay idle in Nate's hand. They were caught in the spell of the story, made real for a moment by Echo's low, clear voice and well-chosen words. There was silence when she had finished, as the sailmaker slowly pulled the thread through his sail and another curled shaving joined the pile around the boy's feet. Echo, who herself had forgotten the existence of the shop and almost of her audience, sat without speaking, watching the dust motes caught in the sunshine from the open door float in the air.

"Thank you, lass," said the sailmaker, breaking the silence at last. "That is a fine story and well told."

Echo flushed and looked down at her feet. While she was telling a story, she was never self-conscious, but she did not like to be the center of attention afterward.

"If I was the Fool," Nate remarked emphatically, now that the spell was broken, "I would have told the king to build his own flying ship before I let him back in the castle."

"It was still the king's castle," Echo remarked mildly. "You are right, of course, the king was neither a kind man, nor a man of his word. But still, his castle."

"Do you suppose the Fool's friends lived at the castle too? Or do you think they went on to have more adventures and help other people?"

"I expect they stayed for a little while," said Echo, smiling.

"But not forever. They were the sort of people who are made for adventure."

She turned to the sailmaker, deciding that it was time to come to the reason for her visit. "Sir," she said, "I would like to buy a sail. Or at least, a large piece of canvas. Squarish would be fine, although it does not need to be any particular shape. Do you have anything in a dark color?"

The sailmaker reflected for a moment. "I do have what's left of the canvas from that wreck that was salvaged a few months back," he said. "Doing a bit of smuggling, I think they were. The sails are dyed a dark brown. How big would you need it to be?"

Echo did some quick estimation in her head and gave him a number.

"I reckon this piece of canvas would be about that," the sailmaker said. "I'll bring it out and you can see if it's what you're wanting." He stood up and went through a small door at the back of the shop, where supplies and extra sails were kept. Nate set down his whittling and followed his grandfather. The two of them came back a few minutes later, carrying a tightly folded square of canvas that was dark brown in color. They went past Echo, through the open front door, and into the street. "Come on out," called the sailmaker. "We will unfold this, and you can see if it's what you want."

She stepped out into the street, where the sailmaker and Nate were busy unfolding the canvas. Spread out, it was exactly what she was looking for, large enough to cover the moon, and dark enough in color to not be readily visible at night and to hide the glow of the moon. "I'll take it," she said. "Could I buy some rope as well?"

Even folded tightly, the canvas was too heavy and too bulky

for Echo to carry a long distance. If she picked it up, she could stagger with it, and that was about all. The sailmaker looked thoughtfully at the canvas for a moment, then sent his grandson for a wheelbarrow. "There is a shop a few doors down that makes and sells them," he told Echo. "You can get one reasonably."

After a bit of bargaining, Echo and the sailmaker agreed on a price that satisfied both of them and she paid him with the money she had brought from home. Even with the rope, canvas, and wheelbarrow, she still had a little left. Not enough, perhaps, but she would worry about that when the time came.

By this time, Nate had come back with the wheelbarrow. He and his grandfather heaved the canvas into it, and Echo tucked the ropes into a corner. She waved goodbye to Nate and the sailmaker, having already thanked them for their help. Then she lifted the handles of the wheelbarrow and trundled off down the street.

Out of sight of the shop, she turned into a little alley and stopped. She unslung her pack and rummaged around in it until she found her scarf. Grimacing a little, she tied it over her hair in the manner of a village woman's kerchief. Instead of putting the rucksack back on her shoulders, she tucked it into the wheelbarrow before starting off again.

She made her way along the street, maneuvering the wheelbarrow in and out of the waterside traffic, trying not to get in anyone's way. Sailors and porters carrying crates and bales were harder to dodge now. She also kept an eye on her pack to see that no one snatched it. Eventually, she reached the city wall and another gate, the river gate. It was wide open at this time of day, and Echo pushed her barrow through it unhindered. She turned to her right, moving away from the river and keeping near the city wall.

She was on the west side of the city, so, unfortunately, the wall did not provide any break from the afternoon sun. Echo could feel it hot on her shoulders as she bent over her load. Sweat trickled down her back, and the hands that clutched the barrow handles were damp with it.

After walking for a while, she was beyond the city, taking a dusty track between green fields. The scent of crushed ragweed, growing untidily along the side of the road, filled the air. There was a breeze here, away from the city, and it helped a little to dispel the heat. Corn grew green and high in some fields; cattle grazed in others. Echo noted the richness of the ground. That came from being near a river, she supposed. She had always heard that bottomland was the best.

She was headed toward the trees, but it took her a long time to get there. She had to walk through several miles of fields, and the wheelbarrow seemed to grow heavier with every step. After a time, she stopped noticing her surroundings and simply plodded along, thinking of nothing more than putting one foot in front of the other, until, finally, she reached the woods.

She had not been noticed or challenged. Used to working quietly and unobtrusively, avoiding notice by seeming to take no notice of things around her, she moved openly, focused on her work, and because she did not act suspicious, she drew no suspicion. No one paid any attention to another farm girl, her hair tied up, working through the heat of the day. There seemed to be enough coming and going, even away from the city, that a stranger was not remarked.

Once well into the shelter of the trees, Echo promptly stopped the wheelbarrow. She took her scarf off and shook her hair loose. There was no denying that it could be a nuisance sometimes, especially when working, but she still preferred that to having it bound up. She stuck the scarf back in her pack and picked up her burden again.

Getting the wheelbarrow through the woods was more difficult than pushing it along a cobbled street or dusty track. She had to manhandle the heavy load over roots and rough ground, shoving with her knees as well as her hands, sometimes. She maneuvered around trees and larger rocks. The woods were somewhat rougher on this side of the valley than the side she had come from. The shade was nice though, and there was no traffic here.

Echo stayed close enough to the edge of the woods that she could glimpse the city from time to time. She kept her eye on it when she didn't need to look at the ground, using it to judge her position. When she caught sight of the hunting gate, the one she had seen from inside the city that morning, she stopped. She looked around until she found a tree that was taller than its neighbors to use as a landmark and parked the wheelbarrow near it.

After taking a few moments to memorize the position of the tree and the surrounding area so that she would be able to find it again, Echo left the wheelbarrow and scouted around the nearby woods. Eventually she found a shallow cave which she thought would suit her purpose. It was almost directly downhill from the hunting gate, deep enough in the woods, and there was a stream nearby, which was nice.

She retrieved the wheelbarrow and tucked it away in a corner of the cave. Sitting down on a convenient rock just outside, she rested her tired feet and aching arms. It was not so hot anymore, she realized. The shadows were long and slanting, and the breeze held the cool of evening. It had been a long day, and she was very tired. And very hungry, she realized suddenly. She had had nothing to eat since early morning. She remembered feeling hungry around midday, but she had been busy and ignored it. That was so long ago she had almost forgotten.

It was too late now to get back to the city before dark. Too late to steal the moon tonight. Echo decided that that was just as well. She would have time to rest first and would not need to steal the moon while she was exhausted. Leaving food a little longer, she went down to the stream and bathed. She put on the other dress from her pack and washed the one she had been wearing, spreading it out on a bush near the cave to dry. Then she chewed slowly on some dried meat and fruit from her pack as the sun set over the valley. Before the long summer day had quite reached its end, she had tipped the canvas out of the wheelbarrow, unfolded it enough to make a bed, and was fast asleep upon it.

* * *

Echo walked along the dusty track toward the city. The slanting afternoon sunlight warmed her skin through the cloth of her dress. Grasshoppers whirred lazily in the weedy verges at the side of the road. A cart rumbled past, the driver flicking flies off the backs of his horses in a desultory fashion. Even the swishing of the horses' tails was half-hearted. It was another hot day, and everyone was feeling too drowsy to bother much about anything.

Echo herself could not recapture the nervous energy of this morning. She had woken early and puttered around the cave, cutting branches to screen the opening, double checking that she had everything in her rucksack, checking the distance to the hunting gate a hundred times. There wasn't really anything very useful for her to do, but she tried to keep busy until the time came to go back to the city. By midafternoon though, her energy had worn away with the heat and drowsiness of the day, and her nervousness with it. She did what she needed to do now, but she was no longer keyed up over it. Steadily, but unhurriedly, she made her way to the main gates of the city. Another cart or two passed her, and once a foot traveler, but there was very little traffic at this time of day.

When she reached the city, Echo paused a moment outside the enormous double gates. They were open now, so she could not see the emblem of the bird and the flames as she had the morning before. She looked up to the tower of the castle, where the pennant fluttered in the wind. The rays from the lowering sun turned the bird to fire, the flame to gold. The air felt cooler, suddenly, as the sun, on its pilgrimage to the other side of the world, took its warmth with it. She touched the warm metal of the gold medallion around her neck and took a deep breath, a little of her nervousness returning. Then she steadied herself and stepped through the gates and into the city.

Finding the courtyard with the moon was easier this time. The way seemed much shorter, now that she had traveled it before. The streets were quiet, but the courtyard of the moon was still full of people. Echo paid her penny and slipped to the back of the crowd. The sightseers' eyes were on the moon, and the guards' eyes were on the sightseers. Echo found a spot next to one of the trees and waited quietly until the crowd was shifting, as one group left and another came in. Unnoticed in the subdued confusion, she grasped the lowest branch of the tree and pulled herself up. She climbed right into the thickest branches, screened by the green leaves, her brown dress blending with the trunk. She found a stout branch to sit on and waited, shifting her rucksack from her back to her lap. She knew she would have to wait a long time, and that this branch was going to get very uncomfortable. Leaning back against the trunk, she half-closed her eyes, and tried to dream the time away without becoming completely unaware of her surroundings.

The sun sank slowly, setting the sky ablaze with color. The clouds lining the western sky turned orange, then gold, then paler orange. The crowd in the courtyard gradually dwindled until it disappeared altogether. The air grew cooler, but not cold, and in any case, Echo was used to sleeping outside. She eased her cloak out of her pack and wrapped it around her, careful to move slowly and quietly, to make no motion that would draw attention. She stretched her cramped legs, changing her position slightly, and resettled her pack in her lap, resting her arms on it. The pack was inconvenient, especially for climbing up and down trees, but she had not liked to leave it behind at the cave. If things went wrong and she had to run, she would need it with her.

In the distance, she heard the town crier call out the hour, the traditional cry of "All's well," echoing through the city. The gates were closed at this time, she knew, as the last of the sun faded from the sky. No traffic in or out of the city until morning. The guards watching the moon must change at this hour as well, she realized, as another set entered the courtyard. They exchanged a salute and a few words with those who had been there all day, then took up their positions around the courtyard while the first set left, their boots ringing on the stone. Echo roused herself from her dreams and observed the new guards closely.

Two were of middle age and appeared to be veterans. She thought it likely that they had served in the palace for many years and perhaps seen some active service as well. The third was young and was giving his entire attention to the task at hand, anxious to acquit himself well and impress his superiors. The fourth was perhaps about thirty, and he had a long, white scar across one tanned cheek. The sword he carried was curved, while the other three guards wore straight swords. He appeared almost lazy in contrast with the others, but Echo received the impression that he did not miss much. Or perhaps anything. All the guards stood without moving, almost blending into the background, easy to ignore. But that impression was misleading, she knew. There was a watchfulness about them that belied their immobile stance.

The sky darkened, but no torches were lit in the courtyard. The moon shed its soft glow all around, with only shaded corners such as the tree where Echo hid becoming truly dark. She reflected that the guards could probably see better without torches anyway, as they would not ruin their night vision by looking into the light. The shadows, also, would not seem as dark in contrast to the moonlight as to firelight. Which was sensible from the point of view of protecting the moon, but of course made things more difficult for her.

The night wore on, and she dozed fitfully from time to time. She would be resting peacefully, awake but relaxed, and then gradually drift off. When that happened, she would wake with a start as her head slipped to one side, or she felt herself starting to slip off the branch. The last thing she needed was to fall asleep and ignominiously out of the tree. Several times, she woke with a start thinking she was falling, and then realized it was a dream. But she knew it was just as well that she didn't sleep too deeply. Keeping an eye on the time was important. She had decided to wait until a few hours after midnight, when the night would be darkest and the guards at their most weary.

By that time though, Echo was feeling pretty weary herself. She wanted nothing more than to sleep the night through, somewhere she could stretch out comfortably, instead of being cramped up in this tree. But she had a moon to steal. Sitting up, she stretched a little, flexing her muscles so that they would not cramp when she went to climb down. She shifted her pack to her back, then listened to the noises of the night, trying to bring her senses to alertness. She was careful not to listen too long to any one sound, not wanting monotony to send her back to sleep. When she felt a bit more awake, she slithered down the tree in the dark, careful not to break any branches or make any noise that would give her away.

The night was still, which was rather a pity. Wind would have helped to mask any sound she might make. She would just have to be more careful. Thoroughly awake now, she felt alert and fresh, all her sleepiness gone. Adrenaline rushed through her veins, making her feel as aware and full of energy as if it was a beautiful morning after a good night's rest, instead of a little past midnight after a few hours in a tree. She worked her way around the edge of the courtyard, staying in the shadows. Quietly, carefully, she moved unhurriedly, sometimes no more than an inch at a time, knowing that nothing draws the eye so quickly as movement. When she had positioned herself so that the moon was between her and the courtyard entrance, she paused.

All she had to do now was make a rush at the moon and shove it hard enough to knock it off the pedestal, where it would roll out of the courtyard, smash through the hunting gate, roll down the hill, and come to a stop in the woods. Then she could escape in the confusion, beat the guards to the bottom of the slope, roll the moon into the cave, and cover it with the canvas before the guards found it. It was a fairly simple, straightforward plan, which meant there was less to wrong, but she knew there were some holes in it.

This is stupid, Echo thought. *If any one of those guards is even half a woodsman, he'll know immediately where the moon is. It won't just roll down the hill without leaving a trace, not to mention the tracks I'll leave getting it into the cave.* But she didn't have any better ideas. For half a moment, she considered calling it off, slipping back out of the courtyard, out of the city, away. She could do it easily enough. She wouldn't have to deal with the moon and all the trouble that came with it. She could just keep going, wander on, see the rest of the world. But she knew she wasn't going to. It wasn't in her to leave without trying.

She set her mouth in a way that anyone who had known her grandfather would have recognized. It was an expression that Owen wore when he had been warned that something was impossible, but he intended to do it anyway. Then she took a breath, and leaving the shelter of the shadows, dashed across the open space towards the moon. The light grew brighter with every step she took, the soft but brilliant glow of the moon spreading across the grass and pavement. Reaching the pedestal, she set her shoulder to the moon and heaved with all her strength.

Chapter Four

The surface of the moon was cold to the touch, much colder than might have been expected after such a warm day. It seemed to have soaked up no warmth from the sun, only light. It was a curious texture, almost like stone, but smoother and hollower. There were bumps and dips on the surface, but no rough edges. She lifted the hand that had touched the moon and brushed her fingers together. A fine, milky dust drifted from them, glowing for a moment, then fading.

Remembering the job at hand, she tried bracing both hands against the moon and shoving. It hadn't budged at all the first time. Now, it rocked slightly. She shoved again, setting up a rhythm, rocking the moon so that it tilted farther each time. Somewhere behind her, Echo heard the shout of a guard and running feet. She had been noticed, although it had taken them long enough. Then she realized that less than a minute must have passed since she had run into the light. It felt like longer. But they still should have noticed her sooner. She gave a final, desperate heave, and the moon rocked forward and toppled from the pedestal. It hit the ground with a soft thud, then rolled quickly out of the courtyard, just as she had intended, leaving darkness behind it.

Echo felt someone behind her and twisted to one side, sheltering along the wall in the thickest shadows. She edged toward the entrance. It would not be long before someone found torches, and she needed to be out of the city by then. There were shouts and running feet. She took advantage of the confusion and dashed out of the courtyard. From the street, she could see the moon's progress down the slope by its own light. It was a silver-white blur in the darkness, growing smaller with each second. She ran for the hunting gate as more guards pounded down the street behind her, a few carrying torches. They were heading for the courtyard, and she hoped she was too far away for them to see in the darkness, and that they were too distracted to notice her. Even as she ran, she thought that it was silly of them to go into the empty courtyard, rather than after the moon. Maybe they hadn't seen it, either, and were just running to where most of the confusion seemed to be.

The shattered ruins of the hunting gate loomed about her in the darkness as she ran through. The splintered wood and jagged edges reminded her of some of the smashed trees in the forest where the moon had first fallen. She dodged one broken piece of wood, leapt over another, and then her feet were brushing through grass instead of scraping over stone. She was outside the city walls. Something that had been tense in her loosened. Avoiding the guards would be easier in the open, and her plan had worked so far. The moon was out of the city, and so was she. She darted to one side without slackening her pace. She would need to circle around, out of the path of the guards who would soon be coming after the moon, to reach the bottom of the slope. And she needed to get there before they did.

A figure rose suddenly out of the darkness, too suddenly for her to stop or even swerve out of the way. She collided sharply with leather and metal, and for a moment it felt as if all the breath had been knocked out of her body. Winded and dizzy, she stumbled back. A hand of iron gripped her upper arm. Recovering a little, Echo twisted and kicked, struggling to free herself. She lashed out with her free arm but hit nothing. She was being held at arm's length and there was nothing to hit at except the hand that held her. And she could not break the grip.

Light appeared in the broken gateway. The man holding Echo snapped a short order and the torches moved closer. He did not speak loudly, but his voice cut through the noise of the searchers. In a moment, Echo and her captor were surrounded by guards. Several of them still carried torches, and in the flickering light Echo could see that it was the scar-faced guard, the one from the courtyard, who held her arm. He must have left the courtyard before she had and waited outside, knowing she had to come that way.

The scarred guard motioned with his head, and another guard detached himself from the ring and took Echo's other arm. She stopped struggling, then. It was useless, and therefore pointless. She could do herself no good now and would probably only earn herself a clout if she kept it up. The best thing to do was wait and watch for her chance to get away. Four or five of the remaining guards grouped alertly in a half-circle around Echo and her captors. Another contingent, she could not tell how many in the dark, set off down the hill to recover the moon. Only a few moments, and order had been restored, confusion had vanished, discipline prevailed.

The guards marched Echo back into the city, through the splintered timbers of the ruined gateway, over the rough cobbles, past the courtyard that had held the moon. They continued a little further down the street, then turned into a hidden alley under the shadow of the castle. The alley was narrow, with high stone walls on either side. It ended abruptly in a tall, wooden door, which one of the guards unlocked and swung open. They all marched through, the guard relocking the door behind them. Echo realized they were now within the castle walls.

She had not spoken since her capture. She had not screamed, either, only fought silently, reacting half on instinct. No one had spoken to her, either. She had half-expected to be questioned, but except for the iron grip on her arm, she might almost not have been there at all, for all the notice the guards took of her. Maybe attempted moon stealing was an everyday occurrence.

Even though a second guard held her other arm, the scar-faced guard never once relaxed his hold on Echo's left. Her fingers were almost numb, the circulation cut off by that terrible grasp. She would have bruises on that arm tomorrow. Assuming she lived that long, of course. She stumbled in the dark, her feet scraping roughly over the cobbles, and for once she was glad that she was wearing shoes. At least, she thought with grim humor, there was no way she could fall, not held on either side as she was.

The little procession marched through another courtyard, several winding passages, and two more doors. The night was quiet, the tread of heavy feet on stone the only sound. They came to a fourth door, which the key-carrying guard also unlocked. Echo's step faltered at the entrance. This door was different. Instead of another passage, a staircase led down into the darkness. A dank, unpleasant smell rose up to meet her, an underground smell, but not like the cool, earthy one of the root cellar at home. This smelled like a trap, like a grave. They were taking her to the dungeons. She had to steal herself not to struggle again. It would do her no good. She had to make herself keep moving her feet all the long way down. If she didn't walk, she would only be dragged. But it was the hardest thing she had ever done. Much harder than entering a strange city alone. Harder than taking that first step to steal the moon.

She wanted to scream and fight. She wanted to tear herself out of her captors' hands, beat herself against that unmoving wooden door at the top of the stairs. Like a wild animal that will struggle wildly and unreasoningly when caught in a trap, until the trap breaks or it does, she wanted to fight her way free. She wanted to do anything to keep from taking one more step.

She did none of those things, though. Instead, she kept putting one foot in front of the other, all the way down those stairs, just as if they were any other steps she had taken since the beginning of her journey. She pushed down the fear that rose in her stomach, refusing to give way to panic. She kept her back straight and her shoulders back, allowing none of her terror to escape her. Because she was Echo of Pebblestone, and she still had a job to finish. This didn't end until the moon was back in the sky.

They traveled downward for a very long time, or so it seemed to Echo. At some point, she realized that she should have thought of counting the steps, so she would know how far she had come. It was too late now, though. And perhaps it was better not to know.

At last, they reached the bottom, and then there was a wait. She looked around and saw that they were in an irregular stone room, lit by torches placed in brackets along the walls. There were no cells here, no other prisoners. Echo realized it was a guardroom. Bunks lined the walls, a few occupied by snoring guards. Other guards were engaged in a quiet game of cards. One of these was dispatched with a short order. Echo did not quite catch the words, but she figured it was to get someone in authority that would tell them what to do with her. Meanwhile, one of the group who had escorted her in occupied the time by searching her pack. Not either of the ones who gripped her arms, unfortunately.

The searcher removed her knife, but left the rest alone. Echo was grateful for that. When she got away, she was going to need her things. The other guards had relaxed a little, in the safety of the dungeons with four solid doors between their prisoner and freedom, but not the scar-faced guard. In all that time, his grip never shifted nor slackened.

When the head jailer came in, summoned to deal with the new prisoner, the thought passed through his mind that the prisoner and that one guard looked curiously alike. They both stood straight, silent, stone-faced, in the flickering torchlight. Both apparently indifferent to their surroundings, but watchful. It was a silly fancy, however, and the jailer immediately dismissed it. Prisoners and guards were entirely different. It was only sensible.

The head jailer was slightly grumpy anyway about being awakened at this time of night. He had worked out a very good system for where to put prisoners, and the guards should have known what to do with this one. At the same time, however, such inconveniences were part of his job, so now that he was awake he took it philosophically. Still, as it wouldn't do to let this sort of thing continue, he berated the guards just the same.

The scar-faced guard listened impassively. It was his job to guard the moon and capture anyone who messed with it. It was not his job to decide what to do with prisoners. That was the head jailer's job, and how the head jailer did it was no concern of his. The scar-faced guard didn't say all this, but his demeanor said it for him.

The other guards, however, were suitably chastened, and it was one of them who explained what Echo had done and asked what was to be done with her.

"Put her next to the other one," the head jailer said briefly, and went back to his interrupted sleep.

The procession set off again, down winding passageways lit by flickering torches. There were cells on either side now, and through the barred doors Echo could see the recumbent forms of prisoners. Hopefully they were just asleep. Probably new prisoners being brought in was such a common occurrence that it didn't even disturb them. She was taken straight through what she guessed to be the main part of the dungeon to the other side. There were fewer cells here, some partly hewn from living rock.

At last, they stopped in front of an iron grill door. The guard with the keys stepped forward again and unlocked it, swung it open. Echo was maneuvered to the threshold, although none of the guards stepped inside. Only then did the scar-faced guard release his grip. In the same moment, one of the others pushed her in. She stumbled and fell to her knees, hearing the door clang shut and the key turn in the lock behind her. The guards' footsteps moved away.

She sensed movement to her right and looked up. The cell had a second occupant, and he had bent down and was reaching out a hand to help her up. She took the hand automatically. It was large and square and deeply calloused. He pulled her to her feet, and it was only then that she realized that there were bars between them.

Taking stock of her surroundings in the dim light that filtered through the door from the torch in the passageway, Echo saw that what she had taken to be one cell was actually two, divided by a row of bars down the middle. The bars were closely spaced, hardly wide enough for the other prisoner to reach his arm through. Her own cell was made up of stone walls on two sides, the bars on the third, and the door on the fourth. It was deeper than it was wide, and not very big. There was a bench along one wall and a pile of straw in the back corner. The second cell was a mirror of her own.

Then she looked at her next-door neighbor, who had been watching her get her bearings. She couldn't see him very well in the shadows, but she could tell that he was tall and big, with shoulders as square as his hand had been. The stranger spoke. "Not much to it, is there?" he asked cheerfully. "Mikkel of Blue Fjord, at your service," he added.

"Echo of Pebblestone," she returned politely.

Mikkel leaned against his own stone wall. "What brings you here?" he asked conversationally.

Echo took her pack off and set it at one end of the bench. She removed her cloak as well, bundled it up, and set it on top of her pack. "Half-a-dozen guards and a miscalculation." She pushed her hair out of her face and sat down next to her pack. "You?"

"Something similar," Mikkel said. He sat down on his own bench, six paces away on the other side of the bars.

Echo laughed. "I already know what you did."

"Really." He leaned back against the stone. "And what is that?"

"Same thing as me," she answered ungrammatically. "That's why we are both here. In these particular cells, I mean, as well as in the dungeon in general."

"You tried to steal the moon?" he leaned forward, interested. "What did you do that for?"

"To return it to the sky, of course," she replied, nettled. "Why were *you* stealing it?"

"Same reason." He settled back on the bench again. "So, what was your miscalculation?"

"What?"

"You said six guards and a miscalculation."

"Oh." Echo paused. "I ran right instead of left. He was waiting, that guard with the scar, and he caught me."

"I know the one you mean," said Mikkel. "He was there when I was captured too."

"What was your miscalculation?"

Mikkel grinned. "I got caught."

"Not very clever of you," said Echo.

"No," he agreed, "I will do better next time."

"You are trying again, then?"

"Certainly. Are you?"

"I have to get out of here first." She yawned. "I haven't had much sleep tonight. I'll think about it in the morning." She spread her cloak on the bench, then took her blanket from her pack and wrapped it around herself. She settled on the bench, using her pack for a pillow. "Good night."

"Good night, Moon-thief."

"Moon-stealer yourself," she muttered sleepily, and then she drifted off.

Mikkel settled back on his own bench, lacing his fingers behind his head and staring at the stone ceiling. He had been asleep before they brought the new prisoner in, but he felt wakeful now. He hadn't been here long enough to get sunk in lethargy like some. It was early morning now, and he often got up at this time, or had before getting locked up in here. That was the problem with a place like this, there was no reason to get up. Nothing to look forward to but the next meal.

His thoughts returned to the problem of the moon. He hadn't been the only one to try to steal it, then. Well, it made sense. If he had tried, there would be others. Not to mention the king appropriating it in the first place. He, Mikkel, would need to get out of here soon, though, or someone else might succeed in stealing the moon and disappear with it. Hmm, that might not be an altogether bad idea. Let someone else steal the moon first, someone easier to rob than this blasted city, and then take the moon from them. That would be awfully chancy, though. It depended on another person succeeding in getting the moon, but failing to keep it, and Mikkel hated depending on other people. He would always do things the hard way rather than ask for help. Anyway, other people were often undependable, and the more people involved, the more there was to go wrong. Much better to manage it himself.

His thoughts checked there. This girl, the one they had just brought in, might have something to say about that. He knew stubborn when he saw it, which was also every time he had looked in a mirror. Perhaps it wouldn't be such a bad thing. If she was determined to steal the moon and serious about returning it to the sky, they might be able to work together. He wouldn't be depending on anyone else, then, and neither would she—they would merely be combining efforts for the same purpose. After all, if they both wanted the moon returned to the sky, it would be silly to work against each other.

It depended on the girl, though. She might not even still want to steal the moon. But as soon as he thought that, he knew it wasn't true. She wasn't the kind to quit. She looked—he searched his mind for a word that wasn't tough, because that didn't describe her at all. Resilient? That was it. Unbreakable.

One look and Mikkel had known she was like him, that to be trapped was almost the worst thing that could happen. That she needed open space, room to breathe, almost as much as she needed air. But she had stood there in the torchlight, as brave and straight and proud as any of the guards, and later she had laughed when talking to him. It had been such an unexpected sound in this place. He hoped she would still feel like laughing tomorrow. He wanted to hear her laugh again. Then he wondered if she would be as brave after months down here, or years. He wondered if he would be.

* * *

When Echo awoke, light was filtering into the cell through a grillwork high on the back wall. Compared to daylight outside, it would be dim, but compared to the torchlight of last night, it was brilliant. *It's all in how you look at things,* she thought drowsily. Sitting up rather stiffly, she stretched. The bench was worse than the ground for sleeping on, and probably the stint in the tree the night before hadn't helped either. She checked her left arm, feeling it gingerly. Yes, it was certainly bruised.

She stood up and looked around. The cell seemed even smaller in the daylight than it had by the torches of last night. She stepped it off. Three paces wide by six paces long. Not much for an indefinite stay. She walked back to the end of the cell farthest from the door and examined the straw there. Deciding it was clean enough to risk sleeping on, she folded her blanket neatly and set it on top of the pile. The straw would certainly be warmer and more comfortable than the bench. She folded her cloak, stowed it in her pack, and set the pack next to the bench. After that, there didn't seem to be much to do.

Restless, she glanced through the bars to the other cell. The man was sitting on the floor, chipping idly at the mortar in the wall with a loose piece of stone. He looked up when he felt her gaze. "You're awake," he said.

"What time is breakfast?" she asked him.

"About midmorning," Mikkel told her, "Any time now, in fact. You slept late."

"It was already morning by the time I got here," she said tartly, but without real anger—just as he had spoken without real malice. "Considering how late I got here and how little I slept, it's still early."

He got to his feet with a grin, dropping the stone next to his bench. "You must be hungry," he said. "They bring food twice a day. It isn't bad, but it gets boring after a while. Still, it could be worse."

"Things can always be worse," agreed Echo cheerfully. Food came then, and both prisoners dropped the conversation for the more important business of eating. A guard brought it, rattling along the passage with a sort of trolley. A huge, iron kettle rested on the trolley, full of porridge. In the next cell, Mikkel slid a narrow wooden trencher through the bars. The guard ladled a helping of porridge into it and slid it back. He reached Echo's cell and took a spare trencher from the bottom of the trolley, ladled some porridge into it and slid it through the bars. He handed Echo a spoon with the laconic advice, "Take care of it, you only get one," and moved off down the passage.

"Wait," said Echo, "won't the dishes have to be washed?"

"No need for that," said Mikkel. "They don't feed us enough.

Don't try using the spoon for digging or anything," he warned "You'll be eating porridge with your hands for the rest of your stay." He took his own spoon from an outcropping of rock he had used as a shelf and dipped it into his porridge.

"A guard always delivers the food," he went on. "Less chance of a slip-up that way. An ordinary person is more likely to become friendly with the prisoners. And if a guard makes a mistake, they can always court-martial him."

"Not much chance of that," said Echo. "He doesn't even have to open the door. In fact, he wasn't even carrying keys. What about water?" she added.

"They bring that next. Same way."

Echo found she was quite hungry and ate the tasteless porridge with a good appetite. Between bites, she observed her companion, eating his own porridge on the other side of the bars. He was young, she decided, not many years older than herself. Even sitting down, he was tall. Her first impression in the dim torchlight earlier had been one of height, and she decided that she had not been mistaken. He was big as well as tall, neither gangly nor stout, but well-built. Dark brown hair, streaked with gold where the sun had touched it, fell in shaggy locks across his broad forehead. His eyes were bright blue, alive, intent. He had a strong, square jaw, and straight nose. His face was tanned by weather, with strength and determination written across it.

When Echo had cleaned out her trencher, she set it to one side, near the bench. The guard came back presently, the trolley loaded this time with pails of water, and gave her a second trencher which he ladled full. Echo drank thirstily.

"It has to last all day," Mikkel warned.

With breakfast, the main event of the morning over and done

with, Echo settled herself to put in the rest of the day as best she could. She used some of the old water from her water skin to clean the dishes. Then she paced around the cell a bit, restless, but with nothing to do. Later, she curled up in the straw and dozed for a while, drifting in and out of sleep and between daydreams. Pushing away thoughts of the moon and her captivity, she thought about stories instead. She was exhausted, anyway, from excitement and lack of sleep the last few days, so it was easy to do. The evening meal revived her a little bit, and she puttered around for a while, fiddling with the contents of her pack, doing some more pacing, making up a bed on the straw. When the daylight started fading from the grill, she stretched out on the straw bed and fell almost immediately into a deep and dreamless sleep.

The next morning she woke early, feeling rested and full of energy. Glancing into the next cell, she saw that Mikkel was still asleep. She made her bed of straw as neatly as possible, brushed her hair, and straightened her clothes. The morning chores finished, she looked around for something else to do. Her eyes fell on her pack. She emptied its contents onto the bench, sorting through them and repacking them neatly. When traveling, things tended to get rather jumbled, with stuff she used a lot staying near the top and other things forgotten at the bottom. She missed her knife. It would have been useful when she escaped from here.

Echo hesitated over what to do with the food. There wasn't a lot left to worry about, a little meat, a little fruit, a little flour—the flour wouldn't be much use in here since she had no way to cook anything—some salt, and hardtack. She wondered whether she should ration out the food to liven the prison fare or save it. She would need food when she got away. On the other hand, she would need more than what she had right here, and she didn't want this going bad if she was down here for a while. The food wouldn't keep forever, especially if it stayed damp down here. In the end, she put the supplies back in her pack and decided to wait a few days for developments.

That decided, she turned her mind to the problem of escaping. There didn't seem to be much to do there besides wait for developments either. As things stood, she had no way of even getting out of the cell. And getting out of the cell would only be the beginning. After that, she would need to get out of the dungeons, then out of the city with the moon. She looked over at the next cell again. Mikkel wanted to escape too, so maybe they could work something out together. She had a feeling they were stuck with each other anyway, until the moon was returned to the sky. She intended to see the task through, and from what he had said, Mikkel did too. Well, there were worse people to be stuck on a quest with. He looked resourceful. Echo had never thought that there was anything she couldn't do, but maybe stealing the moon wasn't a one-person job. After all, they had both tried to steal the moon—alone–and they had both failed. Still thinking, Echo sat down on her bench to wait for breakfast.

* * *

"Mikkel, tell me what you know about this place." Echo was sitting on her pile of straw, leaning against the stone wall. She had picked a single straw out of the pile and occupied her hands by bending it at intervals, trying to make them as even as possible.

Mikkel looked up from a design he was scratching on the

wall—Echo thought it looked like a mechanism for raising and lowering a sail—and walked to the back of the cell where he dropped comfortably onto his own pile of straw. "The dungeon or the city?" he asked obligingly.

"All of it." Echo had been a prisoner for three days and she was still thinking about escape. She realized that if she was going to be successful with that, and with stealing the moon this time around, she would need to know as much as she could about the place where she and the moon were secured. She and Mikkel had talked from time to time, and she had gathered that he had done some reconnoitering before trying to steal the moon.

"Right, let's start with the dungeon. First off, there's the head jailer. You met him when you came in?"

Echo nodded. "He seemed strict, a little pompous, but I think he would be kind in ordinary circumstances."

"A fair assessment. His name is Richard, and he is a very methodical man, very precise. He designed the entire system the dungeon runs on. The guards, the food, where to put prisoners, everything. He used to be a soldier, a good one but not a brilliant one. He could carry out a campaign faultlessly if things went according to plan, but he had trouble pivoting with the unexpected. Here, he sees to it that nothing unexpected happens. This is his place, and he is very good at what he does. You saw that with the food system. Not much leeway for escaping there. On the other hand, we prisoners are much better taken care of than we might be under a less organized man. The food is never late."

"The thing about systems," said Echo thoughtfully, "is that if one thing were to go wrong, the whole thing could be thrown into disorder."

"Exactly." Mikkel's grin flashed. "Don't think I haven't thought about it! The trouble is finding a disruption that would end with us on the other side of those doors.

"Anyway, Richard likes everything to be in its proper place. I hear that nothing disturbs him so much as something that doesn't fit. His office is always neat as a pin, his papers are invariably in order, and his prisoners are always where they should be. He has organized these haphazard, rambling, dungeon corridors as well as they can be organized, and he assigns prisoners to cells according to crime. He's got murderers in one section, thieves in another, and so on. They say he sorts through the prisoners and reorganizes periodically, as a child will sort through the buttons in a button-box, putting them in different piles each time. Also, he rearranges as more prisoners are brought in, or as some are taken out."

"You mean—we might get rearranged?"

Mikkel laughed. "Don't worry, *kjære*, he is sure to keep us near each other. He is very organized, remember. And we have committed exactly the same crime."

Echo flushed. "I didn't mean that."

"Mean what?"

"I don't know. Whatever you thought I meant. Tell me about the city."

"Torenia." Mikkel resumed his narrative. "The city was built more than three hundred years ago, and the settlement in the valley has been here longer than that. It grew with the river traffic. The castle was built to protect the valley. Now it controls it. The soil here is rich, and the trade along the river is lucrative. There used to be a good deal of trade from the sea as well, but that stopped over whatever happened with the king's sister, long ago.

"The king is named Prometheus. He stays holed up in his castle most of the time and runs the kingdom from there. His wife died early in their reign. They had one son, killed in a carriage accident along with *his* wife a few years ago. Left a child, a son, the current heir. The boy has never been seen outside the castle. The king tries to keep his family close, not that it's done him much good. There's some story about his older sister running off when he was a child, not to mention his son and daughter in law. They say, though, that the king hardly spent any time with his son or his son's family when he was alive and rarely sees the child even now. He's more interested in collecting rare treasures.

"Which brings us to the moon. When the moon fell, the king immediately sent men to investigate. When he found it could be moved, he had it brought to the city. He cut a whole road through the forest, just for that. Transporting the moon was quite an undertaking, but he spared no expense. And it seems he intends to hold on to it.

"Having obtained his prize, the king protected it well. Torkel—that's the guard with the scar who captured us— was put in charge. Guards are changed three times a day in eight-hour rotations. Torkel is always on the night-shift, sometimes the day-shift as well. Otherwise, guards are never on the same shift twice running. Torkel doesn't want them to get into a routine.

"He's not one of the regular guards, and he's only been here a short time. He is a mercenary, but never disloyal to his current commander. He's fought in a dozen different countries, but never one for very long. Whatever he was hired to do, he does, and then he disappears. He's independent and keeps his own counsel. No one knows much about him."

Mikkel paused and looked at Echo. "You really didn't try to find this stuff out before getting locked up?"

"I pretty much just walked in and rolled the moon down a hill," she admitted. "Getting locked up wasn't part of my plan."

"Maybe if you had had more information, you wouldn't have gotten locked up," he scolded.

"It doesn't seem to have done *you* much good," she pointed out, dryly. "You are in here too. Was getting locked up part of *your* plan? You seem to have found out quite a bit about the dungeons in this information you have collected."

Mikkel grinned, unruffled. "Even the best plans go wrong sometimes."

"It wouldn't have mattered anyway," Echo said, going back to the original problem. "Even if I had known all this, I wouldn't have done anything different." She had continued to fiddle with the straw as they talked, bending it at smaller and smaller intervals, and then breaking it into tiny pieces. Now, she brushed the bits off her skirt and picked out another straw from the pile, beginning to bend that one as well. "I knew the moon was guarded, and guarded well. But I still had to try."

"Still, you should always learn as much about a place as you can," Mikkel advised her. "Before you do anything in it. Especially something as risky as stealing the moon. You never know when the information may help you, and it doesn't do to go walking in blind."

"Walking in with your eyes open didn't help you much," she reminded him again. But she herself knew the power of knowledge. "How does one go about learning these things? How did you find all this out? You could hardly just ask. You would look terribly ignorant or show yourself to be a stranger."

"Taverns are a good source of information," Mikkel said. "A

person can pick up a lot there, just by listening." He glanced over at her and added in a slightly different tone of voice, "I wouldn't recommend you trying that one, though."

Echo had enough sense not to ask why not. She knew he was not disparaging her ability to listen.

"You can ask children," Mikkel continued. "Children always know more than a person would think, especially street children, or pickpockets and suchlike. And while they might be scornful of you for not knowing, they will give you answers, if only to air their own knowledge. Or you can often ask shopkeepers, and beggars can tell you things, if you have a coin. For some things, you have to know what you want to know and ask the right questions. For others, you just have to listen and make use of what information comes your way."

"You have traveled a lot?" She asked, but it was hardly a question.

"All over," Mikkel acknowledged. "By sea and shore and land and mountain. We Northmen are a restless race." He stood up as he spoke and walked about the cell, taking long strides as if forgetting that he was trapped by the walls, that he could not keep going. Brought up sharply at the door, he stared through the bars, but there was nothing to see except the passageway and more stone. He gripped the bars, his knuckles whitening. The lock rattled a little, but the door itself didn't budge. Mikkel relaxed his grip, and walking slowly back to the pile of straw, sat down. "Never mind. I've been in worse situations. I'll get out of here, one way or another."

"I'm sure you will," said Echo, straight-faced. He looked at her suspiciously, but she seemed sincere. "We all will—one way or another," she added, a smile creeping to the corners of her mouth. It wasn't even that funny, but they both laughed.

"Seriously, though," she said after a moment, "You would probably manage an escape if anyone could. Why *did* you find out so much about the dungeons though?"

"I picked most of that up after getting locked up. I wasn't as interested before."

"And how do you know so much about all these people?"

"The king's affairs are public knowledge, one of the dungeon guards told me about his boss, and as for Torkel, I knew him before. I've knocked around a bit, as I said, and our paths crossed once or twice."

"Were you fighting beside each other or against each other?" she asked shrewdly.

Mikkel grinned. "Sometimes one thing, sometimes an-other."

Chapter Five

The days wore away with monotonous regularity. Wan day-light would filter through the grill, and the torches would be extinguished. A taciturn guard would trundle by with food, and a little later, water. The food in the morning was generally porridge. Then, the long hours would crawl past. Late in the afternoon, the guard would return with more food and water. The evening meal was generally a sort of stew. The light would fade, the torches would be lit. You would settle down to sleep, but having dozed half the day, you might end up staring at the ceiling for hours instead.

Echo spent a lot of the time dreaming up new stories and remembering old ones. Her mind had that wonderful—if somewhat dangerous—facility of being able to shut out the outside world and live in one of her own creation, inside her head. She wondered again what people did who had no recourse to their own thoughts. What would it be like to depend entirely on the outside world for entertainment? This was one thing she was glad she didn't know. Telling herself stories whiled away many long hours.

She and Mikkel also talked a great deal. One could have too much of even the most pleasant dreams, and there was nothing more real than Mikkel. He looked and seemed very much out of place in the cramped cell. Always, he moved freely, easily, as one used to striding over open country or keeping his balance on the rolling deck of a ship. He was full of life, very much alive.

Mikkel had no trouble keeping himself entertained either. He was not one to depend on conversation or outside influences any more than Echo. He scratched designs for ships on the walls, studied various charts and maps that he kept in his pockets and pack, or chipped industriously away at his escape tunnel. He had kept working at the spot Echo had noticed him chipping at on the day of her arrival, and the hole was now about the size of his fist. Not, as he admitted to Echo, that there was a great likelihood of being able to escape that way, but it was something hopeful to do. He had no objection to talking sometimes, however. There was a lot of time and not much to do with it.

"Tell me about your home, Echo," he said one day. She dropped the bits of straw she had been playing with into her lap. She had always been able to think better when her hands were busy. Brushing off her skirt, she looked up at him suspiciously. "Why? You're not thinking of raiding it sometime, are you?"

"I would never raid the home of an ally," he assured her solemnly. At least, his voice was serious, but a smile pulled at the corners of his mouth.

"Are we allies, then?" she asked curiously. In spite of the smile, she knew he meant what he said.

"Aren't we? We both tried to steal the moon. And I don't suppose either of us are giving up?" He looked a question at her, and she shook her head firmly. "Then there are really two options," he went on. "We can fight each other for the hazardous privilege of returning the moon to the sky, or, since we both want the same thing, we can work together."

Echo has sort of known this all along. He had just put it clearly into words. So she accepted it easily and stood up to put her hand through the bars. "Allies, then," she said, smiling a little at the repetition of her previous words. He grinned back as he stood, on his side of the bars, to take her hand in his warm, firm clasp. They shook hands and returned to their respective piles of straw. Echo leaned against the stone, looping her hands under one knee. Mikkel tented his fingers behind his head and stretched his legs out in front of him. "You were going to tell me about your home," he reminded.

"Okay, but I warn you there's not much to steal and you'd have a hard time getting that." She smiled to show she was at least half-teasing.

"I can understand that, if they are like you." He was completely serious this time.

"No one there is like me," she assured him, "But they would fight." She began to tell him about the village between the forest and the sea—where she had lived all her life until a few months ago. She told him about the fishing and the small farms, that hard but good life that her people had lived for generations. Then she found herself talking about those people, thoughtfully, and with almost an outside perspective—hadn't she always been something of an outsider?—but with pride in her heritage as well.

"We are proud," she said, "And fiercely independent. We come from an ancient line and acknowledge no man to be our better. The outside world doesn't mean much to most of us— to most of them—the land and sea they live on is big enough because it's theirs. But the people aren't narrow-minded. They just mind their own business. Kings and conquerors, the rise and fall of civilizations—that means nothing to them. Such things have passed them by, and they know such things come and go. What is really important, what will always be important, is what you do to build a good life for your family. The food you put on the table and the people sitting around it. We have this pride and independence born of having to do things ourselves and having no one to depend on. And although we bear our own burdens and never ask for help, we are always ready to give it. We would share our last crust as ungrudgingly as if it did not mean going without ourselves. Part of our pride, I suppose," she added.

She looked up, suddenly realizing she had been talking more to herself than to him. "It sounds rather contradictory," she said, but without any trace of apology, "But then—people are like that."

"I know," said Mikkel. "I think I understand."

"What about your home?" she asked. "What are your people like?"

"I haven't been back there in a long time," he said. "I've been wandering."

"But you still think of it as home—as much as you think of any one place that way," she added.

"Well, it's where I was born, even if most of my life has been spent in other places."

"You can tell me about your 'wandering' later. Just now, I want to know where you come from."

He began by describing the rugged, beautiful country, the high mountains, the tangled wilderness, cascading waterfalls, and deep fjords—especially the one for which his town was named. He talked about the northern lights on a winter night, the icy beauty of a world entirely frozen. "Most of the time, the snow doesn't melt the whole winter through. We go months without seeing the ground, unless we want to dig for it. On the very coldest days, we curl up inside our houses and sleep through the day—kind of like in here," he added, looking around the cell for a moment. "We make up for it in the summer, though," he went on. "The summer days are so long there is hardly any night at all. It even gets hot, at least comparatively, although compared to most of the places I've been, the summer weather there is very mild."

Echo found herself listening to his voice almost as much as his words. Not that she missed anything he said. But she liked his voice. It was deep, and as warm and strong as his hand. He went on to tell her about the town where he had grown up, a town with water—the sea and the fjord—on two sides, and mountainous wilderness on the others. As he spoke, a clear picture of his home and the life there grew in her mind; a place where it snowed through the winter and often rained in the summer; the churned mud of the town streets in front of houses that were rough, but sturdy and warm; the mountains at the back, the open sea to the front, sea that was fruitful, whether from fish or from the plunder of lands on the other side. And the life there, a life where you worked hard, fought harder, feasted heartily, and laughed loudly. A life that was often rough and difficult, but where you lived every moment of it. Where fighting, also, was a way of life, and you learned to hold a sword almost before you learned to walk.

He told her about his father, the captain of a longship, and his mother, a woman gifted with both beauty and sense, who had made their home a happy one. He told her about his brothers, all of whom had followed the call of the sea as soon as they were old enough to have a place on a boat. Several of them were captains now, commanding their own longships, and a few still sailed with their father.

Echo took now from his words that restlessness that he had spoken of earlier, the never-ending desire to explore the wide world—to see what lay over the next hill, beyond the next wave. This was something she understood very well herself. It was why she had left Pebblestone. But Mikkel's father, and his brothers too, always returned home. They might travel long and far, they might love every moment of the journey, but they were always glad to be home. Glad to come back to the ones who waited for them, bringing with them spoils and stories. *That's where Mikkel and I are different*, she realized. *We don't have any roots. We have no one belonging especially to us.* There was loneliness in that thought. But also freedom.

"That's where I come from," Mikkel finished. "I left pretty young though, and I've made my own way ever since. Not because I didn't like it there, but because there was something in the world I had to see, something I had to do. Something I'm still looking for."

"I know," said Echo. "I think I understand." Her lips curved upward in a smile, and the corners of his mouth twitched in answer.

"What do you do in your village, Echo?" Mikkel asked. She could have told him about the garden, about the cows, about the cooking, the spinning, or any of the hundred and one things she did to help keep their lives going. Instead, she said simply, "I tell stories." Because that was the simplest and truest truth about her.

"Could you tell one here?" he asked her.

"I will, later. You can see stories better in the firelight."

"We have torchlight."

"That's what I was thinking."

Later when the torches were lit, she told a story. And in the days to come, she told many more. She had a good voice for storytelling, Mikkel thought, low and clear with just the right amount of emphasis but not so much you were distracted by it. It soon became accepted that once the light had faded and the torches had been ignited, she would tell a story. It was something to look forward to in the dreary monotony of the cell, an escape, for a little while, to long ago and far away. She started with the story of the girl with the silver hands and went on to the one about the devil with the three golden hairs, the white bear, the princesses who danced their shoes away, the golden bird, the flying ship—all the brave old tales she had known and loved for as long as she could remember.

"I like your stories, Echo," Mikkel said once. They had been in the dungeon for some time by then. "They are hopeful. Like you."

It was one of the things he liked about her, that simple and unwavering belief that everything would turn out all right. It went, he thought, with the absence of blame. She did not rail against fate, or the guard who had captured her, or the choices that had brought her here. She accepted what had happened and looked forward to the next thing. It was his own outlook on life, but he had never expected to see it reflected this way in some else. You could look at it like falling off a boat into deep water, he thought. If you sat there and cursed the boat or the water, or whoever had pushed you, you would drown. But if you kept swimming, kept moving forward, you might make it out. Of course, Mikkel had been through enough to know that sometimes everything is not all right—that sometimes things go terribly wrong. But then, Echo knew that too. Perhaps that was the difference, though. She knew it—but he had lived it.

Still, even when things did go terribly wrong, there was usually something you could do, he thought, returning to his usual optimism.

"Really?" Echo was surprised. "Some of those stories are rather sad. And—and harsh." She liked the stories, but she wasn't blind to their darker side. "I mean—they usually end well enough—but think about what some of those people went through! Can you imagine life ever being the same for them again?"

"That's what I mean," said Mikkel. "They endure terrible things, yet it comes right in the end. That's hopeful."

"But when you're right in the middle of it," said Echo slowly, "you don't know that everything will be all right in the end. Things could just as easily go terribly wrong."

It was the same phrase Mikkel had used earlier in his thoughts, and he smiled a little. "That's why we call it hope. Not because we know. But because we believe."

Echo did not tell all the stories. Mikkel kept their tacit agreement and told her about his 'wandering,' as she had said. He didn't tell her everything, or even nearly everything—she knew that. But he told her a good deal. He had traveled all over, as he had said, and had been everything from a shipwright to a sailor, from a soldier to a miner. He had settled quarrels in Argos and started them in Constantinople. This was not the first time he had been a prisoner.

Sometimes the things he told her made her eyes widen a little, but she was careful not to let him see. She liked hearing his stories. Not only were they interesting in themselves, but they also told her a lot about the world and a bit about the teller.

In spite of all the storytelling, they did not talk all the time, or even nearly all of it. They spent hours, sometimes entire days, in the companionable absence of sound. Echo had never been one to talk for the sake of filling silence with empty words, and if she had nothing to say, she said nothing at all. Mikkel, also, saw no need to keep a conversation going if there was nothing to talk about, and he appreciated the lack of idle chatter. He would work on his escape tunnel in peace, pleasantly aware of Echo's quiet, understanding company, and secure in the knowledge that if she did interrupt him to say something, it would be worth listening to. As for Echo, she could daydream as much as she liked without worrying that anyone would mistake her silence for annoyance or ill temper. Mikkel did not interrupt her often, but when he did, it was without apology. She didn't mind though. What he had to say was generally more interesting than her daydreams, and that was saying something.

* * *

In spite of the conversation and companionship, the days dragged by more and more slowly. The weather outside grew hotter, leaving the dungeons stifling and airless, although they never escaped a faint underground chill. Long hours crawled past, with nothing particular to fill them and nothing to look forward to.

Mikkel would scrape at his escape tunnel, which was only slightly larger now, or study one of the charts from his pack. The guards had not taken anything from him except his weapons either—although the larger part of Mikkel's gear seemed to have consisted of weapons. Echo would fiddle with her straw and drift off into dreams—dreams of stories or home, or the outside world, which sometimes seemed so far away. And it was—as far away as the other side of the door.

The dungeon weighed on her soul. It would have been strange enough, being under a roof again after so many weeks under trees and sky, but to be trapped in a stone box, and, worst of all, to know you couldn't leave it, was a thousand times more terrible.

The monotony was broken only by the bringing of food, the lighting and extinguishing of the torches, until these, too, became monotonous. It was hard to tell how much time had passed. Each day was like the one before, with nothing to separate them. Echo and Mikkel agreed that they should have started keeping a tally of the days when they were first captured, but neither of them had, and somehow, they were both reluctant to start now. Mikkel reckoned it was about midsummer by the angle of the sun through the grill, and they left it at that.

One night, Echo felt too stifled to sleep, too caged to dream. She walked restlessly from one end of the cell to the other, until Mikkel turned and said wryly, "It doesn't get any bigger, you know." He hadn't been sleeping either. Instead, he had been standing at the door, staring through the grillwork as if he could see out of the dungeon. Now, he caught himself, and returning to his pile of straw, subsided onto it with a surprisingly graceful motion and stretched his long legs out in front of him. Echo sat down on her own pile of straw on the other side of the bars, tucking her feet under her. It was just as bad for Mikkel as for herself, she knew. He was like her. He needed open space, room to breathe. To look, and see distance. To walk, and not be stopped.

Mikkel leaned back against the wall with a sigh, lacing his fingers behind his head. "Tell me a story, Echo," he said.

She clasped her hands over her knee and began, "Once there

was a poor fisherman..." It was the story of the fisherman who had stolen a star from the sky for the bride he loved so much. Echo had always loved this story, although, she remembered, the last time she had told it had been the night the moon fell. She went on, her low, beautiful voice filling the shadows with the familiar words. Slowly, she relaxed, the tension and worry slipping away, until she too, leaned back against the wall, feeling strangely peaceful. She did not look at Mikkel again until she came to the end, although she was aware of him there beside her.

She was surprised then, to see him sitting upright, every sense alert. He had obviously been listening intently to every word, and her surprise must have shown on her face, for he said, "I know that story."

"You mean you've heard it before?" she didn't understand.

"I mean I've always known it." He looked at her squarely, his face alight with discovery, his blue eyes blazing into hers. "My great-great grandfather stole the star. I didn't realize the story had traveled so far."

"It's true then?" Echo was startled into alertness herself.

"More or less," said Mikkel.

Echo wasn't sure what she thought about that. She had always thought of her stories as long ago and far away. She liked to wonder if they had their roots in fact, if something like that had once happened, but she had never expected to have it confirmed. The thought was rather disquieting. The stories were magic, intangible, unproveable, and therefore could not be disproved. They belonged to her because she knew them and dreamed about them and loved them. That the story was true made it less hers somehow. It didn't belong to her anymore, it belonged to the people who had lived it. And to not only realize this, but to be confronted in the same moment with the uncompromisingly flesh and blood descendant of people she always imagined to be imaginary was definitely disconcerting.

Mikkel, watching her, had read her thoughts with disturbing clarity. He didn't comment, though, only said, "You're missing the most important part, Echo."

"Oh." She was quick to understand. "You know where the path to the sky is." She considered this new information thoughtfully. It made sense, somehow fit. Oddly enough, it was much less startling than learning that her story was true. "Have you been there?"

"No. It is not a journey to be undertaken lightly. But I know how to get there. The knowledge has been handed down in my family along with the star."

"The star?" she was taken aback again. Legends were coming true, when she preferred them to stay legends.

"My mother wears it now," said Mikkel. "Maybe you will see it someday."

"I've seen lots of stars," she said, "but you knowing where the path to the sky is—that will help us when we escape and steal the moon."

"You didn't—I mean, you *don't* know where to find the path to the sky, do you, Echo?"

"No."

"What were you going to do?" he was half amused, half exasperated. "Walk around the world, with the moon on your back, looking for a way to return it?"

She was unruffled. "I would have figured something out."

Serious now, he looked at her, sitting there in the dim torchlight, a slender, indomitable figure. So sure of herself and her faith that everything would work out all right. So strong, and yet so fragile. A slip of a girl, with that unusual beauty and a core of steel.

"I believe you would have," he said quietly.

"I met you," she said. "And you know how to get to the sky. So that part worked out. And the rest will too, if we just give it time."

Mikkel was silent for a few moments, thinking. Then he said abruptly, but gently, "All of us have a breaking point, *kjære*."

"Yes," said Echo, "but there is nothing that can't be endured."

"You are right," said Mikkel, and he rather thought she was. She would never break, so she would never know how close she had come to breaking.

* * *

Hour followed hour, day followed day, week followed week. The summer passed very slowly for the two people trapped underground. Time can seem endless when there is nothing to fill it with. Every day was the same. Light filtered through the grill, the torches were extinguished. Food was brought by a taciturn guard, who grunted when spoken to if he was feeling loquacious. Then water was brought the same way. After that, there was nothing to mark the passing of time or distinguish one hour from another until food and water were brought again in the evening. The diluted sunlight would fade, the torches would be lit. The long, airless nights, filled with the oily, smoky smell of the torches, passed even more slowly than the days.

Echo and Mikkel didn't talk much about the moon anymore, or about escaping. There wasn't much they could do except wait for an opportunity. And as the long days crawled ever more slowly past, the likelihood of that seemed fainter and fainter. It sometimes seemed to Echo as if she had been trapped here forever. As if her journey through the forest in the springtime and her whole life in the village by the sea were no more than a dream. Sometimes, though, it was the dungeon and the aimless, purposeless life she was drifting through now that seemed unreal. Then she would wonder, vaguely, not as if it really mattered, if the cell, if the stone, if she herself really existed. The outside world was even harder to believe in.

When she felt this way, she would look at Mikkel in the next cell, at his serious face, his wide shoulders, the lock of brown hair that tumbled across his forehead. He usually kept busy, chipping at the rock, drawing designs for ships on the walls, or pacing restlessly. Even when sitting still, he radiated life and energy. Mikkel was reassuringly substantial. He was too solid, too practical, to ever be mistaken for a dream. In those days, he was Echo's anchor to the earth.

* * *

When a change did come, it was not a welcome one. There had been no warning to herald it, nothing to distinguish that morning from any other. It had passed with the dreary monotony of so many before it. Echo had awoken as the guard extinguished the torches for the day, but she had not gotten up. Instead, she had lain in the straw with her eyes half-closed, imagining herself to be somewhere other than here. In the forest again, walking through the springtime, the peaceful sameness of the days so different from the enforced routine of the dungeon.

She had finally roused herself when she heard the guard

coming with food, which she ate slowly, more out of habit than hunger. After breakfast, she brushed out her hair and folded her blanket neatly before settling back on the straw. She picked up a piece of the straw and began weaving it through her fingers, watching Mikkel chip at the escape tunnel which was, by this time, the size of his boot. He pulled the bench in front of it, now, when the guards were due to come by.

"I think," Mikkel said, breaking the silence, "that this rock I am digging with is wearing down faster than that hole is growing." He held the rock up for inspection, and Echo looked at it critically.

"It does look smaller than it used to," she admitted.

"I've tried to pry another one loose, but I haven't managed it yet," he said.

"I could see if there are any loose over here," she offered. It was something purposeful to do, and she hopped up off the straw almost cheerfully. She began going over the walls methodically, testing each stone to see if it wiggled, especially the smaller ones. They worked in companionable silence for a while, and then Echo began humming softly to herself. Soon after, Mikkel started to whistle, a tune that had no relation to Echo's, making an agreeable disharmony. They looked at each other and laughed—pleased to have something to do, glad to shake off the gloom of the dungeon for a little while, and happy in each other's company—before turning back to work.

It was a little later that Mikkel and Echo heard the sound of booted feet on stone. That meant guards were coming and usually signaled food. They both knew the sound well enough, having learned to listen for it—as people do who are hungry and bored. Mikkel heard them first and stopped whistling, his work suspended, listening closely. It was not time for a meal, and this sounded like several guards, not just one. Echo had heard them as well, and she turned to face the door. Mikkel dropped the stone he was digging with into the hole he had made, and quickly slid the bench in front of it. He stood up and faced the passageway as well, relaxed, but ready. They waited in silence, side by side with the bars between them.

The guards turned the corner of the passage, six of them, one with the keys Echo had not seen since the night of her capture. For a moment she felt a wild hope. The guards stopped at Mikkel's door. Four of them drew their swords. One stepped forward with a length of rope. "Put your hands through the bars," he ordered.

Mikkel looked them over, thoughtfully, making no move to obey. The youngest and newest guard shifted his feet impatiently and glanced at his superiors, but the others waited impassively.

"We can do this one of two ways," Mikkel said finally. "If you want trouble, you can come in here and try to tie me. Or, you can leave my hands free, and I'll agree not to make any."

The guard with the rope was nettled. "You know we could have a dozen more guards here in five minutes."

Mikkel smiled easily. "I know. It wouldn't matter. The cell's too small for more than a few of you at a time."

The senior guard had been there when Mikkel was captured. He shrugged his shoulders and motioned the guard with the rope to step back. "All right." To the other guards he said, "If he says he won't, he won't." To Mikkel he said, "If you decide to change your mind, you'll get a sword in the gut."

Mikkel grinned appreciatively. A stomach wound meant you took a lot longer to die. "It's a bargain," he replied.

"Stand back until we've opened the door," the senior guard

instructed. Mikkel picked up his pack from the corner and waited while they unlocked the door, swung it open, and the guard with the keys stepped back behind the ones with the swords. He looked once at Echo, smiling a little wryly. "I'll be seeing you, Moon-thief," he said.

She nodded tightly, unable to speak.

"Come out, slowly," the senior guard directed, keeping his sword ready. "Now walk—I'll tell you when to turn." Mikkel walked down the passageway with the guards behind him. In a moment, he was gone, and only the guard with the keys was left, relocking the door. Then he, too, went after the others, whistling cheerfully, and Echo was alone. She sat down slowly on the bench, staring through the bars into the emptiness of the next cell.

* * *

The other cell was not left empty for long. A day or two later, Echo heard the guards' boots again, this time accompanied by the shuffling feet of a prisoner. There were only two guards this time, and neither of them had their weapons drawn. The prisoner wasn't even tied. Looking at her, Echo was not surprised. The woman looked long past trying to escape—or even wanting to. About her was an air of passive hopelessness, as if she had gone through despair so long ago that she had forgotten what it felt like and no longer cared. When the guard unlocked the door, the prisoner shuffled in and sat down on the bench. The guards relocked the door and left.

Echo observed her new fellow-prisoner, although she guessed that "new" was a relative term. New to the cell perhaps, not the dungeon. This prisoner looked like she had been down here a long time. Echo found it hard to judge her age. She might have been very young, or again, quite old. The gray in the pale hair that hung lankly about her face might have been from age, or it might have been from dirt. She had stooped when she walked, but that might have been from apathy as well as age. Her clothes were ragged, and also tinged with gray, in this case almost certainly from dirt. A loose pair of downtrodden slippers were on her feet. Her hands rested listlessly on her knee.

"Hello," said Echo tentatively, her voice sounding loud in her own ears. She spoke in a lower tone, as seemed to befit the quietness of the cell. "They'll be bringing food and water in a little while. Are you thirsty? You could share mine until then."

The woman gave no sign that she had heard. She never moved at all, just sat there staring at the ground as if nothing else existed anymore. She had never once looked up, and Echo couldn't see her face with the hair hanging over it. She seemed not to even be aware of Echo's presence in the next cell. Echo thought that she must have been down here a long, long time. Long enough that she had stopped caring. About anything. *I wonder how long it will take me to be like that?* she thought despondently. *But then, I didn't know her before. Maybe she never cared in the first place.*

The next week or so had a dampening effect on Echo's spirits. The depressing company of the woman in the next cell was a poor trade for Mikkel's cheerful, reassuring presence. Mikkel made a person feel that everything would be all right. The new prisoner made you feel that nothing had ever been right, and worse, that it didn't even matter. She never spoke once the whole time. All day long, she sat on the bench, not moving. When the torches were blown out, she drifted back to the straw to sleep, or at least lay down. She ate what was brought her, slowly, uncaringly, as often as not seeming to forget the food halfway through.

Echo gave up trying to talk to her pretty quickly. It was worse to talk, receiving no response, than to get along in silence. Echo was used to silence anyway, usually appreciated it, but the despairing presence of the other prisoner got on her nerves. She, who once would not even have admitted to *having* nerves, much less that anything would get on them.

These days though, every little thing irritated her. The sound of the trolley in the mornings and evenings, the scrape of the spoon on the iron pot as the guard dished out food, the smell of the torches, of the cell, the scratchiness of the straw, the hardness of the bench. She felt trapped, suffocated, closed in. She felt like screaming, shrieking, throwing herself against the bars if she had to stay here one minute longer. But she didn't.

She wondered if feelings even existed if they remained locked inside you. To all outward appearances, she was calm and rational. She got up in the morning, brushed her hair and straightened her blankets. She ate, and she moved around the cell. She kept her clothes neat and her possessions in order. No one knew what she felt inside, all the wild thoughts that ran through her head. No one would ever know what she felt right now except herself. And even she would forget, or half-remember, wondering why she had ever felt or thought anything so silly. What she felt right now would never change anything for anyone. It would never matter.

Sheer stubbornness, as much as good sense and a strong will kept her going. Kept her from giving vent to what she felt. Kept her from giving way to despair. She went on, much as she always had, using the very routine that irritated her as a means of stability. Determinedly never letting go of at least the hope of hope, because she had made up her mind not to, not because there was any material reason for it.

When the guards came again and stopped at her cell, she felt a vague relief. At least she was getting away from here. Once she would have preferred this cell to any other in the dungeon. But Mikkel was gone now. It was nothing but a trap.

Two of the guards had their swords drawn, but they didn't tie her hands. It didn't matter too much. Fighting was a game she wouldn't win, and running was equally useless. She hadn't forgotten all the locked doors or the abundance of guards between herself and freedom, even if she knew which way to go.

She was taken up and down two or three passageways and around several turns. She had no idea where she was or even what direction she was going. The excellent sense of direction that served her so well outside disappeared as soon as she was between walls, and she found that she could get turned around very quickly. Before stealing the moon, she had never been in a building big enough to get turned around in. Before coming to Torenia, she had never even seen one.

The guards stopped before a cell that was much larger than the one Echo had been in before. There were over half a dozen people in it already, sitting on piles of straw around the edges. The third guard drew his sword as well, before the fourth unlocked the door. He opened it just wide enough to admit Echo before motioning her through. She didn't know why they bothered. No one in the cell even moved, and she herself had no intention of facing one sword, let alone three. She was reluctant to enter another cell, though. It had been nice even walking along the narrow passageways, nice to stretch her legs a little, nice to see farther than six paces and a stone wall. But she went. They would only push her in if she didn't.

Some of the prisoners were talking quietly, most were just sitting. Two seemed to be playing some kind of game involving dice, small pebbles, and marks on the floor. A few looked up un-interestedly as Echo came in, then went back to whatever they were doing. She stood, taking stock of her new surroundings as the locks clicked into place behind her. There were both men and women in the cell, grouped on opposite sides. Echo cast her glance quickly over the former, but Mikkel was not among them. The men were shackled, she noticed, either at the wrist or ankle with long chains that allowed some movement, while the women had the freedom of the cell.

Echo stepped farther in, picking her way to an unoccupied pile of straw against the back wall. No one spoke to her or even looked up again. Perhaps prisoners came and went too often for them to bother, or perhaps, like her previous cellmate, they had stopped caring. Maybe they were suspicious of strangers, although suspicion seemed too lively a word to apply to this lethargic bunch. She sat down miserably on the straw, huddling with her arms around her knees, feeling very much alone.

Chapter Six

There were eight prisoners in the cell besides Echo. Four were men, three were women, and there was one child, a little girl, the daughter of one of the women. None of them talked much. Two of the men muttered occasionally over their dice game. The third spoke only to complain about the food. The fourth rarely moved at all, and Echo had never heard him speak once. He simply sat there, taking no part in anything. He was an old man, with white hair and surprisingly keen eyes beneath his bushy eyebrows. Echo had the idea that he missed very little, in spite of his seeming indifference to his surroundings.

It was from one of the women that she learned the small history of the cell. The woman's name was Ida, and she seemed the least affected by her surroundings. She was sonsy and good-natured, selfish, but kindhearted. She took things as they came, and here, at least, she was fed. After Echo had been there a few days, Ida decided she was staying for long enough to talk to and proceeded to talk to her.

Ida was there for stealing five chickens from the market. She chuckled when she told about it. "I don't suggest stealing chickens if steal you must," she advised Echo. "They are hard to move, bulkier than one might expect, and impossible to keep quiet."

Echo wondered what Ida would say if she asked about the best way to steal the moon, but refrained.

The child was named Ana, her mother, Rita. Rita had stolen three yards of cloth, and when she was captured had said that Ana had helped her, to keep from being separated from the child. Even the dungeon was better than leaving Ana alone on the streets or letting her be taken to an orphanage, Rita thought.

The third woman was named Bessie, and she was also there for stealing. In fact, everyone in the cell was, with the possible exception of Andrew, the old man with the keen eyes and bushy eyebrows who never moved or spoke. No one knew why he was there. He had been in this cell through the coming and going of many prisoners, but he was never moved. There were speculations and tall tales as to what he had done and how long he had been there, but no one knew for sure. Andrew never said, and no one quite wanted to ask him.

The two men playing the dice game were Gavin and Tom, and the one who muttered about the food was Horatio. Gavin was a housebreaker, Tom a highwayman, and Horatio a pickpocket.

The next several days passed with the monotony that was part of the dungeon. Ida occasionally chatted with Echo, usually to relate some anecdote from her questionable past. She was one of those people who can rattle on indefinitely given an interested listener, or one who can't get away, but Echo didn't mind. Ida's cheerful chatter was a vast improvement to the mournful silence of her previous cellmate. Also, Ida displayed no curiosity whatever about Echo's life, or what had led to her being imprisoned. Whether the lack of questions denoted lack of interest or an unexpected politeness, Echo was grateful for it. She was content to let Ida do most of the talking and had no desire to explain about herself or the moon.

Bessie was too uninterested and Rita too distraught to talk much. Ana kept close to her mother and was very quiet. Gavin and Tom played their interminable game of pebbles and dice, Horatio continued to mutter about the food, and Andrew went on not saying anything to anyone. Ida herself was silent more often than she spoke. She seemed talkative only by contrast. All of them spent more time staring blankly at the wall than doing anything else.

Echo took to staring at the wall herself, not dreaming, hardly thinking, just wishing the time away—if anything so passive can be described as wishing. She felt unaccountably depressed, and for once she made no attempt to talk herself out of it or focus on the bright side. Instead, she hugged her sadness around her like a blanket.

The mood lasted until one afternoon, when Echo awoke from her lethargy enough to feel tired. Tired of the dirt, the walls, the hopelessness on everyone's faces. Tired of waiting, tired of sitting on straw, tired of the same old food every day. Most of all, though, she was tired of not doing anything, of feeling like there was nothing she could do.

Her lips tightened in a way that was curiously reminiscent of her mother. It was a look that had always warned naughty children to straighten up or scatter for cover. Echo had not been the recipient of it for years, but now it was directed against herself—and the situation in general. She moved squarely to the middle of the cell and started to speak.

She told a story, as she would have told one in the village, as she had told them for Mikkel. She spoke as if she were not hemmed in by stone walls, as if she were under the stars instead of under the earth. And as she spoke, the walls ceased to matter, and the cell became a tiny hut in the far north, where wind and storms surrounded it day and night and hunger was never far from the door. It was a castle of ice, where a white bear lived, and a girl who had sacrificed herself that her father, mother, and eight older brothers and sisters might not starve. The prisoners left the cell and journeyed with the girl to the far corners of the earth and the four winds on her search for the castle that lay east of the sun and west of the moon.

There was never much noise in the cell, but now even the low murmurs of desultory conversation ceased. Gavin and Tom's dice lay idle. A guard who had been sweeping in the passageway swept slowly and still more slowly and then stopped altogether. At first, all those in earshot hung on to every word. Later, they forgot to listen, there was no need to listen consciously, as they, too, became part of the story.

The story ended, but the silence remained as everyone returned slowly to earth. Echo slipped back to her corner. The guard began sweeping again, softly, as if still afraid to make any noise. Gavin picked up the dice. Rita gently combed out her daughter's hair with her fingers and began braiding it. Echo leaned back against the wall. She was still tired, but it was a more peaceful kind of weariness. And she no longer felt quite so hopeless.

* * *

She told a story every evening after that, as she had in the village. The flickering torches were a little like the flickering firelight on the square. For a little while, everyone could forget where they were. It gave the prisoners something to look forward to, and Echo something to do. Something tense in her soul loosened a little.

More slow days drifted past. Echo wondered if it was still summer outside. She thought it must be, but she wasn't sure. She thought of her village. How had the crops turned out, without the moon to guide the planting? From what she had seen growing in the valley of Torenia before she was captured, they might have done all right. Had the villagers learned to sail without the tide, managed to catch enough fish for trading and to eat through the winter? She knew they would manage somehow—they always did—but this winter might be a hard one.

She leaned back against the wall, her hands motionless in her lap, her thoughts drifting away like leaves in the wind. She felt too tired to hold them, too worn out even to think. Perhaps half an hour passed as she stared sightlessly at the wall. The heavy tread of guards' booted feet in the passageway hardly disturbed her. Only when they stopped at the cell and one of them began to unlock the door did she look up, suddenly wary.

There were six guards, five with their weapons drawn, one with the key, and in the middle, his hands tied, was Mikkel. His usually untidy hair was more tousled than ever, and one cheek was bruised and cut. Echo also noticed that one guard had a black eye while others sported a collection of cuts and bruises. Three of the guards who had been there when Mikkel was moved several weeks ago were of the group, but the senior guard was not there.

The door swung wide, and the key guard stepped back. One of the others sheathed his sword and shoved Mikkel by the elbow into the cell. A second guard followed, keeping his sword at Mikkel's neck. The others stayed outside and closed the door. Echo was tempted to jump up immediately, but carefully stayed where she was. Mikkel, meeting her eyes as he looked over the prisoners, gave no outward sign of recognition.

The two guards guided Mikkel to an empty shackle on the men's side, and the unarmed one bent to secure it around his ankle. In spite of the sword at his throat, Mikkel was tempted to knee the bending guard in the chin before he had a chance to fasten the shackle. Echo saw the thought pass through his mind and gave a real smile for the first time in weeks.

Mikkel refrained, the shackle was fastened, the guards left the cell and locked the door behind them. Echo came swiftly to her feet and crossed the room to Mikkel. She set to work on the rope that bound his hands. The knots were tight, and it took her a few minutes to get them untied.

Mikkel studied her face while she worked. She was thinner, he noticed, her cheeks hollower than when he had seen her last, but what disturbed him most was the look of apathy that he had noticed from the corridor before she had seen him. It was all wrong for Echo to look like that. Echo, who carried a light inside her. Echo, who was unbreakable.

She was aware of his scrutiny but kept her eyes on the rope under her fingers. "You've had a bad time of it, haven't you, Moon-thief," he said finally. "I was hoping they had let you out."

"No such luck," she muttered, feeling tears suddenly pricking behind her eyes. She did not say how glad she was to see him, how much brighter things seemed now that they were together again. She gave a final tug at the rope, and it came loose from his wrists and dropped to the floor. "There." She looked up and met his eyes squarely now, smiling a little. "You either, I see?"

"Not a chance." Mikkel gave her his old grin. "I did try to talk some of the guards into letting me go just now, but they weren't convinced."

"So I gathered," she said dryly. Then with a speaking glance at his split cheek and battered knuckles— "Are you sure it was talking you were doing?"

He grinned. "I didn't promise not to make any trouble this time around." Stooping, he picked up the piece of rope that had bound his hands and tucked it into his pocket. One never knew when a rope might come in handy. A good sailor was never without one if he could help it. Echo returned to her spot, looping her hands around her knee. She felt more cheerful than she had in days. Mikkel settled down across from her, stretched his long legs out in front of him in an easy movement that hardly rattled the chain, and clasped his hands behind his head. "So, what is there to do around here?" he asked.

* * *

A shout of laughter from the other side of the cell made Echo look up quickly from the straw tower she was building with Ana. Mikkel was playing the dice game, along with Gavin, Tom, and Horatio, whom he had somehow convinced to join. It was Mikkel who was laughing, and Echo's own lips curved upward in a smile at the sound. She looked around the rest of the cell. It somehow seemed like a much less depressing place since Mikkel had been added to the prisoners. The dice game was much livelier, the other three women were chatting quietly among themselves, and Andrew—well, Andrew was much the same, but Mikkel would address a good-humored remark to him now and again, never seeming to mind that he didn't respond.

Echo placed another straw on the tower, then Ana placed the

next one. The tower grew slowly until it was nearly a foot high and slightly shaky. "Now for the fun part." Echo smiled at Ana. "Are you ready to knock it over?"

Ana smiled back, shyly, and tugged swiftly on the straws at the base on the tower. The entire tower of straws tumbled to the ground. She smiled again, wider, and looked back at Echo. "Again?" she asked. Echo picked a straw from the scattered pile, smoothed out a place on the floor, and started another tower.

When Echo and Ana were about halfway through the second tower, Mikkel left the dice game with a cheerful word to the other players and settled back into his usual place. From his pocket, he took the rope that had bound his hands and began to untwist it. Still building the tower, Echo watched from the corner of her eye as Mikkel first took apart the strands, then spliced them together end to end. Next, he doubled the ends over, and, taking a string from his pack, bound the doubled rope together to form handles on each end. When Mikkel finished, she saw that he had made a skipping rope.

The second tower was finished now, so Echo let Ana knock it down again, and this time, before Ana suggested starting another, Mikkel came over to them, as close as his chain would allow. "Have you ever had a skipping rope?" he asked the child.

Ana shook her head, her eyes wide. Eagerly, Echo jumped up and crossed the floor to take the rope from Mikkel. "Here," she said, bringing it to Ana and placing her hands on the handles. "You hold it like this..."

Mikkel returned to his seat and let Echo show Ana how to use the skipping rope, smiling as he watched them together. Ana, her face flushed and serious, her eyes eager, Echo, eyes sparkling and excited. After showing Ana the basics, Echo sat back down and let her practice on her own, smiling as the child skipped around the cell, humming to herself. Everyone else, with the exception of Rita, was pretending not to pay any attention, but they were smiling too.

The next day, Echo showed Ana some of the games that the children played in the village. She had never played them often, and not at all for a long time, but the rhymes were easy to remember, or to make up if you forgot. Mikkel held one end of the rope, Echo the other, and they swung it in a slow rhythm for Ana to jump across. Echo sang,

"Mabel, Mabel, set the table.

Just as fast as you are able.

Shake the salt and shake the pepper.

Who will be the highest stepper?

Winds blow hot and winds blow freeze,

How many times did Mabel sneeze?

One, two, three, four..."

Ida began to clap the rhythm, nudging Rita who joined in hesitantly, almost as if afraid to make any noise. One after another, the others, except for Andrew, joined in as well. Ana leapt back and forth, laughing now, her hair flying. When Echo got to ten, she stopped to rest, breathing hard and still smiling. Everyone laughed, as pleased as if they were on a picnic with their own families on a summer afternoon, when laughter comes easily for no reason at all. A guard, passing by in the passageway, stopped short in astonishment at the unusual sound. No one noticed him.

* * *

Midsummer came and went, unnoticed by the prisoners deep

underground. Life in the cell went on very much the same, but a little more cheerful, a little more hopeful than it had been a month ago. Gavin, Tom, Horatio, and Mikkel played the dice game. Ida, Bessie, Rita, and Echo talked and fashioned dolls out of straw and bits of their own clothing for Ana to play with. Ana played with the skipping rope and her ever-growing family of dolls. Andrew sat in his corner. Mikkel studied his charts, plotting courses to the places he would go, wondering what lay beyond the edge of the map. Echo told stories.

Mikkel had noticed that three or four guards always seemed to be in the passageway when she was telling one. They appeared to take no notice of the prisoners, but were careful to make no noise. The same guards were never there two days in a row, so Mikkel figured they had a schedule worked out where a few could be off duty at that time, and they took turns. Mikkel, who had been a guard at one point and time (although not in a dungeon) and knew how dull it could be, reckoned that they probably looked forward to the stories almost as much as the prisoners.

He would have been amused, although not surprised, if he had known that the guards never talked about the stories or the fact that they listened to them among themselves. The arrangement to take guarding duties in turn was a tacit one, but none the less strong for that. None of them said a word about it, but not one of them thought about breaking it.

Even deep in the dungeons, the afternoons were warmer now. Most of the prisoners tended to drowse through the time until supper, finding it as easy to sleep then as during the slightly chilly nights. Sleeping was still the most common way of passing the time in any case. It was one such afternoon when Andrew, who always seemed to be as alert as he was unmoving, suddenly turned his head and looked straight at Echo. "Come here," he said, not loudly, but as if he expected to be obeyed. "I want to talk to you."

Curious about what he wanted, as he had never spoken to her or anyone else as far as she knew, Echo obligingly crossed the cell and took a seat on the straw near him.

"You tell many stories," the old man began.

"Yes," she said noncommittally, still waiting to see what he wanted to talk about.

"Today, I shall tell you one," said Andrew. And without further preamble, he began to speak.

"Once, there was a great city, ruled over by a great king. He was a proud king, and busy with affairs of state. He had two children, a son and a daughter. The king's daughter, the princess, was some years older than her brother. Being very much occupied with war and other matters, the king saw little of his son and even less of his daughter. She grew up without him knowing very much about it."

Andrew spoke in a low voice, so that only Echo could hear, level and even, so as not to disturb the slumberers.

"However," he continued, "when the princess was kidnapped by the king's enemy, the king grew very angry. He was very proud, and the abduction of his daughter was an insult to that pride. The surrender of the king's city was demanded in exchange for the safety of the princess, but that was a price the king was unwilling to pay. He called on all the heroes in the land to rescue the princess, offering her hand in marriage to the one who could return her safely home.

"In the meantime, the princess had been taken aboard a ship. There was a young sailor on this ship. He had nothing to do with the kidnappers, but was simply one of the crew, a young man in search of adventure. He saw the princess and she saw him, and they fell in love.

"The sailor overcame the kidnappers, and together, he and the princess escaped in one of the ship's boats. After a long and difficult journey, they reached the city. The princess was afraid to return, afraid she might never leave again, but the sailor only laughed. 'You want to see your family,' he said. She admitted that she did. 'And you shall,' he told her. And he promised that they would be together forever. 'A king is only a man,' he said, 'and no man can keep us apart.'

"When the sailor heard that the king had offered his daughter's hand in marriage to the man who rescued her, that made things even simpler. 'Even a king must keep his word,' the sailor told the princess."

Andrew stared straight ahead, his eyes far away, seeing into the past.

"He was a brave, laughing, reckless man, the sailor. He would have walked into the devil's lair and tweaked the demon's nose for the adventure of it. I saw him when he came into the great hall with the princess, both of them ragged and dirty. I was a guard at the time, on duty there. The place was in an uproar, but the sailor threw back his head and laughed and walked straight up to the throne. 'Sir,' he said to the king, 'I have rescued your daughter. I shall marry her as soon as she likes.'

"The hall went silent, everyone waiting to see what the king would do. He stood up. 'That will be never,' he said. 'She has no wish to marry you.' He said it with all the pride of his lineage, but the sailor was undisturbed. That day, it was as if the king stood in front of an equal.

"'Of course I do!' cried the princess, before the sailor could speak. 'I love him!' They faced the king together, hand in hand.

"The king's face went hard with anger. No king likes to be contradicted in front of his entire court. And now that the princess was safely back in the castle, he had no intention of letting her marry a common sailor, promise or no promise. But he did not allow his anger to cloud his thinking. He *had* passed his word, and, publicly at least, he must seem to honor it. And his daughter was obviously infatuated with the man. 'Very well,' the king said. 'But as he is of humble birth, he must first prove his worth.' The king turned to the sailor. 'A pirate has recently been attacking my ships. Bring me his head and return the gold he has stolen'—here the king named a fabulous sum—'and you shall have my daughter's hand in marriage.'

"The sailor had his own opinions about the humbleness of his birth, but he didn't think enough of the king to bother arguing about it. 'Very well,' he said to the king. And more softly to the princess at his side, 'I will return.' He kissed her before them all and left.

"The sailor was gone for many weeks. Day after day, the princess waited. She knew he was coming back to her. He had promised, and so he would come. Then one day he did come, sailing up the river in the captured pirate ship full of gold, the pirate captain's head in a sack which he handed to the king. The king ordered the gold to be counted, and when the counting was finished, the sum was less than that the king had named. It was whispered along the docks afterward that several bags of gold had slipped into the deep water of the river. For though it went hard with the king to lose even some of the gold, it went harder to give his daughter to this man whom he still considered a common sailor.

"The king declared that the sailor had kept some of the gold for himself. He ordered the sailor to be bound in chains and thrown in the dungeon, to be executed the following morning. But when they came for him at dawn, the sailor was gone. So was the princess. No trace of either was ever found.

"The king grew harsher and angrier than ever. He forbade the name of the princess to ever be mentioned in the kingdom. And when the young prince, the princess's little brother, grew up and became king in his turn, he upheld the edict. He had been a child, and deeply hurt by his sister's leaving. So the princess was never mentioned, and people's memories being what they are, was all but forgotten, by all save a few."

Having finished his story, Andrew was silent. Echo sat silently also. She knew why he had told her the story, but she was unsure what to say now. Finally, she said, "That is rather sad. That they forgot her, I mean."

"Is it?" asked Andrew.

"Perhaps not," said Echo. "Andrew," she asked, "why are you here?"

"Because I said her name," he answered. "The name of the princess that was not to be spoken. I spoke it, so that it should not be forgotten altogether. Shall I tell you her name?" He suddenly turned his gaze on Echo, and she stared unblinking into the sharp old eyes.

"I think," she said carefully, "that I should tell you."

Andrew waited, and Echo said slowly, "The name of the princess is Raya." And then more softly, "I am her granddaughter."

Both were silent for a while, and then Echo said, "I have one question."

"So have I," said Andrew, "but ask yours first."

"Tell me what she was like," said Echo. "When she lived in this city, when she was young."

"She was beautiful," he said slowly, his eyes looking into the past again, "but that wasn't what one noticed about her. "She was—magical." He paused. "There is no other way to describe her. When she came into a room, it brightened. When she laughed, the world laughed with her. She was like a star. Beautiful, shining..."

And far away, thought Echo.

"We all worshipped her," added Andrew, "the whole palace."

After a time he said, "Tell me what she is like now."

"She is happy," said Echo. She suddenly felt like crying, though she did not know why. Gently, she touched Andrew's wrinkled hand, then moved back to her own part of the cell.

She sat there, staring at nothing and fingering her grandmother's medallion. She understood the story better, perhaps, than Andrew who had been there. For one thing, she knew her grandparents. There was also her storyteller's instinct, that insight that enabled her to see things that no one else saw, that she would seem to have no way of seeing. Echo understood why Raya had fallen in love with Owen, though he was only a young sailor. *We all worshipped her*, Andrew had said. But Owen had seen her as a woman, not as a princess. He would have seen the faults that no one else thought of looking for, the virtues that no one else thought of noticing, because they thought she was perfect. He had seen *her*, and he had loved her, and to Raya that mattered more than anything.

Mikkel watched Echo, curled up in her corner, thinking. He had not heard the story, but he had seen her listen to it. Being Mikkel, however, he asked no questions. If Echo wanted him to know what had been said, she would tell him when the time came.

* * *

It was nearing the end of summer before King Prometheus, having been informed that his dungeons were nearly full, sat in judgement. Whenever the dungeon became too full to admit more prisoners, the king would hold judgement in the great hall and have a grand clearing out. Various sentences would be executed. Or, if the king decided that a prisoner had served sufficient time for his or her crime, the prisoner would be released. Sometimes he would decide that a prisoner needed to serve a longer sentence and send him back to the dungeon. Even so, the dungeons would be nearly emptied, and the whole process would begin again.

Mikkel and Echo became wary and watchful, waiting their turn. Groups of prisoners had been passing their cell at intervals for several days, only a few coming back. Neither Mikkel nor Echo intended to come back. They had had enough of the dungeon. In low voices, sitting cross-legged on the straw, they discussed what they were going to do.

Echo had told Mikkel what Andrew had told her, about her grandmother who had once been a princess of this city. He had listened thoughtfully, making no comment. Afterward he said, "Look, Echo, if this gives you a shot, then take it. And don't worry about me for at least a week or two. As long as I am sent to a work camp or something, and not back to the dungeon, I should be able to get away pretty quickly. I'll find you."

"What if you don't?" Echo argued. "What if I don't hear from you in a week or two?"

"Then use your position as granddaughter of the princess to have me released," he suggested with a smile.

"That's a risk in itself," she pointed out. "Telling the king who I am, or rather, who my grandmother was, could land me in an even worse position, you know."

He grinned at her. "If it's something you can't handle, I'll come get you out."

She grinned back. "I know. We'll get out of here, one way or another."

"One way or another."

Echo had already known what she needed to do, even if she didn't want to. She would rather have taken her chance at the judgement than make a claim of family, preferring to do things on her own than to involve anyone else. But this was her best chance, not only to be released from the dungeons, but also to stay near the moon. She might not like it, but she would take it. Mikkel knew all this. Of course, he always knew what she was thinking. And oddly enough, she didn't mind from him. Because he not only knew, he understood.

They were both waiting with unaccustomed impatience for their turn. Usually easygoing and unruffled, the long days of inactivity had stretched their endurance to the point that even a few more hours seemed unbearable. But they bore it. The other prisoners were jittery as well. No one liked the dungeon, but for some, the alternative could be worse. Rita picked nervously at her dress and kept Ana close to her. The other women sat in strained silence, as if talking would bring the threatened danger closer. Tom and Horatio watched the passageway, while Gavin stared at the wall. Andrew sat unmoved. He had seen too many prisoners come and go over the years to really worry about anything. Echo paced around the cell or fidgeted with the straw. Mikkel, with careful precision, went through his pack, stowing as much of its contents on his person as possible. Echo knew he was taking precautions in case they took it away from him.

He looked calm, but she caught him putting the same chart in his pocket three different times and knew he was just trying to keep his hands and his mind busy.

The sounds of guards and moving prisoners came closer. Three cells down. Two cells down. The next cell. It was midafternoon before their turn came. As usual, several guards waited outside with drawn swords, in case anyone felt like trying to escape. Three came into the cell to chain the prisoners' hands. They chained the women first, then the men, before unlocking their leg shackles. The prisoners were herded out of the cell and marched in a rough line down the passageway. Echo worked herself into a spot just behind Mikkel. She looked over her shoulder as they left the cell, and the last thing she saw was Andrew, sitting alone on his pile of straw.

The walk seemed as long as the wait had been. The passageways twisted and turned, until they eventually came to a staircase. It was not the same one Echo had been brought in by. Seemingly, the dungeon had at least two exits. The uncomfortable feeling in the pit of her stomach had disappeared when she started walking, and had been replaced by a lightheaded, dizzy feeling. She tried to think of the present and the immediate future and what she would say to the king, but she couldn't seem to focus. *Thirty-five, thirty-six,* she counted the stone steps. *Or was it forty-six?* She didn't remember. *They should wash these steps more often. I suppose there is no point, with prisoners going up and down them all the time. Was that a breeze? It would be nice to feel the wind again.* She thought of the evening at the beach before the moon fell, with the wind blowing freely around her. And the days after that, when she had not been under a roof for more than two months. *Sunlight, I miss sunlight...* How long had she been in the dungeon?

She looked at Mikkel's broad back, just ahead of her in line. No one would guess from the way he walked that he had been a prisoner even longer than she had. Echo straightened her own shoulders, held her head a little higher, and concentrated on putting one foot in front of the other with careful precision.

The air grew lighter as they climbed higher. She could hear voices ahead now, even over the rattling of chains and shuffling of feet. They had reached the top of the third staircase and were traveling through more corridors, much cleaner, wider, and better lit than those of the dungeon. They passed through a shaft of sunlight from a window set high in the wall, and Echo closed her eyes, lifting her face to it. The line slowed. Peering around the people in front of her, she could see wooden double doors standing open, and beyond them the great hall, crowded with people.

She passed through the doors and the noise of many people talking at once hit her full force. Families of prisoners, witnesses to crimes, interested spectators, courtiers, nobles, prisoners, king—the hall was full. It was longer than it was wide, with a high, arched ceiling. The king sat in a raised dais at the far end, judges and councilors around him. Rows of tall windows on each side of the hall, set high in the wall and deep in the stone, let sunshine in. It poured over people's heads in long, slanting lines. Dust motes danced in the light. Echo thought she had never seen anything more beautiful. She ignored the people and drank in the sunlight.

The line moved slowly. Each prisoner was brought to the foot of the dais, where he knelt before the king and then moved to one side while his case was judged. The case was read, witnesses were called, and the prisoner was given an opportunity to speak. The king would confer with his councilors and then pronounce judgement. Echo mostly ignored the droning voices as the hours went by. She did perk up her ears when Rita's case was heard and was glad to hear that she and Ana were both released. Ida and Bessie were somewhere behind her in the line.

Then it was Mikkel's turn. He stepped to the clear space at the foot of the dais as the other prisoners had done, but unlike the others, he did not kneel. He stood straight, shoulders thrown back, head held high, and looked directly at the king. The nearest guard moved forward and said to Mikkel in a low voice, "Kneel. You must kneel to the king before your case is heard. He's the one with the crown, if you're not sure. Go on."

Mikkel remained stubbornly on his feet. The guard was not an unkind man, but he knew his duty. He reversed his spear and struck Mikkel across the back of the knees with the shaft. At least, that is what he meant to do. Instead, Mikkel, in one smooth, continuing motion, hopped over the spear as it came at his legs from behind. A flick of his foot brought it within reach of his chained hands, and the guard's grip, already loosened from the unexpected lack of resistance, broke. Mikkel held the spear, and the guard looked as taken aback as if he had meant to pick up something heavy, and instead it had weighed nothing at all and hit him in the face. The whole thing had taken less than two seconds.

The king, annoyed at the delay and the commotion, leaned forward. "What is going on?" he asked the guard, ignoring Mikkel. "And why does that prisoner have a spear?"

The guard pulled the shreds of his dignity around him. "Sire, the prisoner refuses to kneel."

Mikkel appeared relaxed, holding the spear almost casually, but Echo could see that he was alert and ready, and that he stood determinedly in his original position.

This time the king did look at Mikkel. "Kneel," he commanded. "Do you not know that I am the king?"

"I am Viking," Mikkel said. "I kneel to no man."

The king turned dismissively back to the guard. "Put him with the clearing crew," he commanded. "If he does not kneel, his case shall not be heard. A few months of felling trees may bring him into a more respectful frame of mind. At the end of that time, he shall have one more chance to state his case." The king raised his voice. "Remove this prisoner, he is delaying the judgement! And someone take that spear away from him."

The guard held out his hand for the spear and Mikkel gave it to him without comment. Another guard, the senior one who had moved Mikkel the first time, stepped forward and raised an eyebrow at him. "Well, Northman, do I need to tie your hands as well as chain them?"

Mikkel grinned at him. "Not so long as no one pushes me." He turned and began to walk back down the hall, the guards around him. As he passed Echo, their eyes met for a moment, and then he was out of sight behind her. She did not turn around to watch him out of the hall. It was her turn, and she was stepping forward.

Chapter Seven

Her head was suddenly clear, and so was the space around her. It was not until now that she got her first real look at the king. He was sitting on a throne at the top of the dais, straight and proud, with no sign of stooping. A circlet of gold was around his head. His eyes were sharp, and his hair was white.

She stepped up the first step of the dais, then the second and third, before anyone could stop her. She looked the king straight in the eye. "I shall not kneel before you either, Uncle," she said. She curtsied instead, then, with a single, smooth motion, took the medallion from around her neck and held it out to him in her chained hands. Slowly, never taking his eyes from her face, the king reached forward to take it. Echo held his gaze. The king looked carefully at the medallion, then back at Echo, scanning her features. He looked at the medallion again. Then he turned to the guard at his right and gave an order in a low voice. Echo only caught the end of it. "...and take those chains off," the king had said.

The guard motioned Echo forward and she followed him. He took her out of the great hall, not through the big, double doors she had entered by, but through a small door near the dais. She was glad not to have to walk past all those people again. The corridor outside the great hall was quiet and still. This time, there was only a short walk before the guard opened another door and directed her into an empty room. He unchained her hands and went out, leaving her rubbing her wrists and looking around her. The room was small, and rather bare. It was dusty and had an empty, unused smell. A table and a few chairs stood in the center, a sofa to one side. A tapestry covered one wall. The guard had locked the door behind him, and there were no windows. She was still a prisoner of sorts, it seemed.

Echo figured the king would be a while. There were a lot of prisoners in the great hall to judge. She sat down on one of the chairs, picking one from which she could see the door. Feeling tired, she leaned back and closed her eyes. But she couldn't go to sleep now. Things had only just started. She would have to be ready to talk to the king when he came in. Would he believe her when she explained who she was? Would it even matter? From all accounts, he still held a grudge against his sister. Maybe he would send her back to the dungeon. Or the mines. If she was lucky, she might get sent to the forest with Mikkel and they could escape together. Did they send women to clear wilderness? Probably not. What should she say to the king? That would depend on what he said first. She would have to play it by ear.

Several hours passed before the lock turned again and the king stepped into the room. Echo hopped to her feet and waited, letting him speak first. He was frowning, but looked disturbed rather than angry. After a moment, he said abruptly, "You cannot be Raya's daughter."

"I am her granddaughter, Sire," said Echo.

The king was still frowning. "Then I would be your great-uncle."

"That's true." She smiled at him. "But 'Uncle' sounded

better. A thing can lose its significance through too many words."

"You don't look much like her," the king said critically. "Only your hands and your hair, and the way you hold your head."

"I look a little like my mother," Echo told him.

"You look like him, too." This time the king's frown was darker. By 'him' Echo knew the king meant Owen.

"I look like my father also," she said. Her father, who was Owen's son.

"Why did you come here?" the king asked. "To give me news of my sister, after all this time? To claim some sort of an inheritance?"

"To steal the moon," she said with a grin. "Didn't they tell you?"

"What does the moon have to do with you or Raya?" He seemed confused, and she didn't blame him. "Did you know where it was, and who I was, before you came? What did Raya tell you?"

"When the moon fell, it was a disaster to our village." Maybe she was exaggerating a little bit, but it couldn't hurt. Perhaps he would let the moon go, and this would be easy. "I set out to find it and return it to the sky. I found the spot where it fell, and tracked it here, through the forest. I knew nothing about this place. I didn't know where Raya was from. I didn't even know your name."

"Then how did you find out? And why say anything?" he questioned further.

"I had the medallion," Echo said. "The symbol was on the gates, the flags. It made me wonder. And then I heard a story. As for why—" she paused. "I wanted to stay out of the dungeons, for one. And I think that Raya meant for me to say something."

"But how could you know—you said she never mentioned me." He hesitated. "She is—still alive?"

"Yes, of course," Echo hastened to assure him. "Alive and well and happy. I think she meant for me to meet you, because she gave me the medallion. She wouldn't have done that if she hadn't wanted me to know. And if she wanted me to know, she expected me to do something about it."

The king was still confused. "If she knew where the moon would be, knew you would have to come here, why not just tell you instead of letting you search through the forest?"

"I don't think she knew anything about the moon," Echo explained, "that is my quest. Only that I would find my way here eventually. That I would find her past—and mine, and the family she left behind. She sent me, in a sense, for a reason."

"Well," the king asked, "and what is that reason? Why are you here?"

She laughed. "When I figure that one out, I'll let you know."

"So, what happens now?" he asked then. "Do you want to continue your journey? Stay here? Are you expecting to be recognized as princess?"

"Please, no," said Echo. "All I want right now is some food that is not stew or porridge, and a hot bath. After that, I would like to stay for a little while, if you don't mind. Not for too long, I'll have to be on my way before winter, but maybe by then I'll have figured out why Raya sent me. And I can't leave without the moon, you know."

"You may be my great-niece," the king said, "but I am not giving you the moon just because you ask for it."

She smiled again. "I didn't really ask, did I? But we can worry about that later."

"Very well," said the king. "I'll send someone to find you

a room and bring you something to eat. As you say, we can talk later. In the meantime, you are free to come and go as you please, except in the courtyard of the moon." He left, and the door remained unlocked.

Echo waited a few minutes to give him time to turn a corner and then went out into the corridor. She had had enough of windowless rooms. She went to the nearest window and stood in the light from it while she waited, staying where she could still see the door of the room. She wanted whoever the king sent for her to be able to find her easily.

It was a little while before anyone came along. Echo was sitting down by this time, on the floor, since there was nothing else in the corridor to sit on. She was leaning against the wall, still in the patch of sunlight from the high window. She had closed her eyes and was almost half asleep when the sound of footsteps made her look up.

A girl had stopped at the door of the room Echo had left and was raising her hand to knock. She was around Echo's age, with red cheeks, a cheerful demeanor, and a mass of curly black hair that was escaping from its pins.

"Over here," said Echo, getting to her feet.

"Hello, miss," said the girl. "My name is Peggy. I'll take you to your room, now, if you like."

"Very much," said Echo. "Lead the way." She followed Peggy through a maze of corridors and up several staircases, wondering if she would ever be able to find her way around this place on her own. Her sense of direction, which worked so well in the wilderness, always deserted her the moment she was behind doors. It had never mattered before, of course. All the buildings in her own village were too small to get lost in.

Peggy stopped finally, in front of a door on an upper floor in a quiet wing of the castle. She opened it and stood back to let Echo go first. Echo stepped inside, hardly noticing the room's fine furnishings or the fact that it seemed large enough to contain her family's entire cottage. What she saw was one of the large windows, open, and close enough to the floor for her to see out. All the other windows so far, the ones in the great hall and in all the corridors, had been set too high in the wall for her to do more than sometimes catch a glimpse of the sky.

She ran to the window immediately, not hearing Peggy's muffled cry of alarm, and leaned out as far as she could without actually falling. She closed her eyes for a moment, letting the breeze tangle her hair and delighting in the feel of sunshine on her face. Then she opened them to see the surrounding country spread out below her like a map. The stairs must have been even longer than she realized, because she really was very high up. The room was near the back of the castle. She could not see the city, only the roofs and walls of other parts of the castle, part of the city wall, some fields and farms, and beyond them the forest. She could see the path she had taken when she trundled the wheelbarrow with its heavy load of canvas, the trees near where she had planned to hide the moon. She wondered if the canvas was still in the overhang where she had left it. She could even see, beyond the forest, the faint blue tops of mountains. The trees were so tall she hadn't been able to see them from the ground, but she could now. Echo drank it all in as only one who has seen no farther than four stone walls for a very long time can do.

When she finally (and reluctantly) turned away from the window, she saw Peggy looking at her with astonishment. Echo only smiled, though, and didn't try to offer any explanation.

"There is a bath ready, if you like, miss," said Peggy, relieved that the window business was over and she wouldn't need to grab the girl's feet to keep her from falling out, "and I will bring supper up for you when you have finished."

"Thank you, yes," said Echo. "Both of those sound very good."

Peggy showed her the door to the bathroom and then left, while Echo looked around the room. It really was a large room, light and airy and open, the size and the windows giving it a pleasant feeling of space. After the dungeon, it was wonderful. There were tapestries on the walls, carpets on the floors, and a pleasant amount of furniture scattered about, but not so much as to make the room feel crowded. She went through the door to the adjoining bathroom and found the bath waiting and a clean dress laid out and ready for her to put on.

After she had bathed and dressed, Echo leaned out the other window, letting the wind dry her hair and watching the light fade from the sky. Her windows faced north, so she could not see the full sunset, but she could see from the part visible to her that it was a splendid one. It was with reluctance that she pulled her head back in and looked around the room again. Peggy would be back with supper soon, she guessed, and she was certainly hungry.

Echo went to the door and poked her head out, more to make sure it was unlocked and the passage unguarded than for any other reason. The knob turned easily under her fingers; the corridor was empty. Satisfied, she drew back into the room and let the door shut behind her. Anyway, if they did lock it, there were still the windows. She picked up her pack from the middle of the floor where she had left it and set it next to the bed. She would have to see about getting her knife back soon. Hopefully, now that she was sort of part of the household, they would give it to her. Maybe she could get Mikkel's things as well.

Returning to the bathroom, she made a bundle of her dirty clothes and tucked them into an empty cupboard. She would ask Peggy for water tomorrow and wash them herself. Undoubtedly, Peggy could take them to be washed with the rest of the castle laundry, but Echo didn't trust that. She was worried that if her clothes disappeared into the multitude of washing that a place like this must produce, she would never see them again, and she would need her own clothes when she left. The dress she had on now was very nice, but not at all suitable for traipsing through forests and up mountains.

Rubbing the soft material gently between her fingers, she realized that it *was* very nice, finer than anything she had ever owned. She looked around the room again, at the carved furniture, the bright colors of the embroidered tapestries, the soft carpets on the floor. Her eye fell on an ornate wooden box that seemed to have no purpose, and she brushed her fingers over it. She had almost forgotten the importance of having beautiful things.

There was a light tap on the door, and Peggy came in, carrying a tray containing supper. Echo ate hungrily but yawned all the way through. It had been a long day, and she was very tired. She went to bed soon after, snuggling down into the comfortable mattress and pulling the luxurious blankets around her. Reflecting sleepily that this place might not be so bad after all, she wondered, with a little worry, how Mikkel was faring—and then pushed the thought out of her mind. Mikkel would always land on his feet—or if he didn't, he would get right back up—and he wouldn't appreciate her worrying about him in any case. Warm and clean and well-fed, she fell asleep.

Echo awoke early the next morning, feeling refreshed and

well-rested. She hopped out of bed and dressed quickly, then went to the window. If she leaned out and craned to the right, she could see the sky turning pink and gold and orange with the sunrise. She wanted to be outside. Peering downward, she checked to see if there was any convenient ivy growing up the wall like there always seemed to be in the stories, but the stone was bare. Reluctantly, she drew her head back inside. She supposed she could find someone and asked to be shown to a door, but she didn't have a good reason, and she didn't like to advertise her comings and goings. Later, she would explore on her own and find a convenient way out.

Turning back to the room, she found a hairbrush and brushed her hair with energy. Then she made the bed, looked around the room for a broom but couldn't find one, and began to wonder what to do next. She was very hungry by this time, so she decided to go out in search of food. Maybe she could find an outside door while she was at it.

In stories, the kitchens always seemed to be at the bottom of the castle or palace, so she started looking for stairs. For a moment, she almost wondered if she should take her pack with her in case she couldn't find her room again, but decided that was silly. She would make it back here sooner or later. Following a corridor until she found a staircase, she went down it, then down another corridor, and another staircase, and so on until she thought that surely she had to be near the level of the kitchens. After all, she didn't want to go too far and wind up back in the dungeons. She investigated any promising doors she came to as well, but they all opened into other rooms, none to the outside. The castle seemed to be very empty. Either there weren't very many people here, or she had wandered into an unused wing. Maybe some of both.

Changing direction, Echo walked briskly along another corridor, and this time she must have gone the right way, because ahead of her she could hear voices and the clatter of pots and pans. She slipped through a pair of double doors that swung easily at her touch and found herself in the noisy confusion of the kitchen. Almost immediately, she had to dodge a woman carrying a huge pan of rolls, then another with two pails of milk. Most of the food seemed to be prepared in huge pots and pans in vast quantities, with nothing easy to grab for breakfast. Echo edged forward, keeping one eye on the rolls, which seemed like her best bet, and scouting around for butter with the other. Someone shoved a spoon into her hand and told her to stir. She looked down into the pot and saw that it was syrup, being warmed over the stove. Maybe that meant pancakes.

Looking around, she saw where they were being cooked. Handing the stirring spoon to someone else, she snagged a plate and a fork from a stack of drying dishes, purloined several pancakes and a small pitcher of syrup, and escaped with her booty to the corridors. Finding a quiet corner, she sat down and made a picnic breakfast, then returned her dishes to the kitchen before trying to find her way back to her room.

It took a while, and a lot of wrong turns, but she made it eventually, hoping she was becoming a little more familiar with at least part of the castle. She still hadn't found any outside doors. They didn't seem very plentiful, but she supposed that made sense in a castle built originally for defense.

Rather at a loose end, she puttered around her room for a while, pretending it needed straightening. Really, there wasn't much to do. Finally, there was a knock on the door, and Peggy came in with a tray. "Good morning, miss," she greeted Echo. "I brought your breakfast." She set the tray on a small table.

"Good morning," said Echo cheerfully. "Thank you very much." She was already hungry again and didn't mention her trip to the kitchen. Sitting down, she attacked the food with gusto. "By the way," she asked Peggy, around a piece of toast and jam, "could you have more water sent up? I want to wash some clothes."

"I can take them and have them washed for you," Peggy said.

"Thank you," said Echo, "but I'd rather wash them myself if you don't mind. I just need the water."

"Very well, miss," said Peggy, carefully keeping her face unreadable. She was thinking that this girl was the oddest one she had ever waited on. Who would want to do their own laundry when they could have it done for them?

Echo did her laundry, humming happily to herself, and then hung it up to dry. While waiting for the water, she had fashioned a makeshift clothesline out of curtain cords. She had used all the cords from this room, borrowed several more from the empty rooms nearby, and strung them all end to end between two taller pieces of furniture where the clothes would catch the breeze from the windows. When her laundry was clean and drying, she stood back and surveyed her handiwork, feeling quite pleased with herself.

At a knock on the door she turned, expecting Peggy again, but instead it was a page with a message from the king. "His majesty requests your presence at dinner this evening," the page said formally.

"Right," said Echo, "that's fine with me, but you'll have to send someone to show me how to get to the dining room. I haven't figured this place out yet."

"A guide will be provided," the page told her stiffly, and left.

When Peggy came in with lunch, Echo told her, "I won't need

supper in my room, Peggy. I'm to eat with my uncle."

"The king!" Peggy was excited. "I've worked here half my life and never even seen him!"

"Really?" Echo was curious. "Who told you to get my room ready and find clothes and stuff?"

"Lady Madelena. She arranged everything." Peggy returned to the subject of the king. "Aren't you excited? What will you wear?"

Echo wondered briefly who Lady Madelena was. She hastily reviewed Mikkel's history of the city but couldn't remember anyone of that name. Perhaps a sort of noble housekeeper? Echo turned her attention back to Peggy. If she needed to know, she could find out later.

"...and I'll have to do something with your hair," Peggy was saying from the closet where she was already rummaging through dresses. "I know all the latest styles. I don't have much practice, but—"

"Thank you, but no," Echo said kindly, but firmly. "I am not having anything done with my hair. I will brush it, and that will do. I don't like having it tied up." Echo had brushed her own hair since she was two, and she certainly did not intend to change that now.

Peggy was confirmed in her opinion that the not-princess was odd. Why would she want to brush her own hair when there was someone to do it for her?

"That looks like a lovely dress," Echo smiled as Peggy emerged from the closet with her arms full of a soft, dark blue material. "And if you really want to see the king, you could come down with me later. I'll say I asked you to come so you could show me the way back."

"Really?" Peggy's black eyes sparkled. "The other maids will never believe it when I tell them!"

Later that afternoon, when she had put on the dress that Peggy had found and brushed her dark hair into a soft cloud around her head, Echo stood and looked at her reflection in the tall mirror. She was surprised at how different she looked. The dress was beautiful, the dark blue color of the soft, heavy material suiting her perfectly. It fitted, too, clinging to her curves and trailing almost to the floor in long folds. Echo liked the sleeves, in spite of their impracticality. They flared out from the elbow, growing wider to the wrist until they, too, almost touched the floor. Her hands, framed in the enormous folds, looked smaller than usual, almost delicate. The dress made her look taller. Unfamiliar shoes felt odd on her feet. Golden-brown eyes stared back at her from the mirror, as if from a stranger's face.

Clothes did make a difference, Echo thought, staring at her reflection. She felt different, wearing this dress. She moved differently, conscious of the sweeping skirt and trailing sleeves. *If I wore this long enough,* she wondered, *would I become a different person?* She turned abruptly from the mirror, and walking quickly across the room, opened the door and stepped into the corridor.

Another page was there, waiting to show her the way to the dining room. "Ready?" she called over her shoulder to Peggy. "It's time!" They followed the page down the hall.

Peggy looked both nervous and excited, and Echo realized that she was a little nervous herself. She hoped there wouldn't be too many people there. Almost unconsciously, her steps slowed. She had no idea what to expect of a state dinner, and she hated crowds. She brushed the fingers of one hand over the palm of the other, feeling the hard callouses on both her fingertips and palm. From weeding the garden, cleaning fish, even from spinning wool... calluses put there by a lifetime of work that would stay with her all her life. *I am Echo of Pebblestone*, she thought. *Fancy clothes can't change me.* And food is food, she told herself cheerfully, and no matter how they dress it up it all goes to the same place. She grinned at Peggy and walked briskly after the page.

They arrived at the dining room, and the page stopped and knocked once at the door before opening it and announcing Echo. He stood to one side, while Peggy stepped to the other where she could get a good look at the king, and Echo walked between them into the room. She was surprised to see that the king was the only one sitting at the long table. She felt relieved, though. Maybe she wouldn't have to face crowds after all.

The king rose to his feet as Echo approached and indicated a chair to his left. Echo murmured a polite greeting and sat down, noticing the place settings with a return of alarm. There seemed to be an unusual amount of silverware—at least two or three of everything. The table was beautiful though, made out of dark wood, carved, stained, and polished. The plates were porcelain, and the pattern was very pretty. There was a carefully arranged centerpiece of flowers in the middle of the table, a long way away because the table was so long. Echo hoped the food would be served soon. She was hungry.

"I thought there would be more people here," she remarked, by way of starting the conversation.

"I only eat in company on occasions of state," the king said.

"You mean you usually eat alone?" Echo was sorry for him. She thought of her own happy, noisy home, her mother and father, brother and sister, sometimes her grandparents or aunts and uncles and cousins as well, all of them crowded together around the supper table, chattering about the events of the day. "Don't you have family or anyone to eat with you?"

"My son and daughter-in-law did eat with me sometimes when they were alive. And my wife: but she had been dead for many years."

"I'm sorry," said Echo. "I thought—I mean—I heard you had a grandson."

"Children eat in the nursery," said the king austerely.

The first course was served then, and Echo wasn't sorry for the interruption. She picked out the fork she liked best and began to eat.

"Well, I can be company for a little while," she told her uncle cheerfully. "Although I can see that it would be nice to have peace and quiet most of the time. I quite enjoyed being alone while I was traveling."

The king did not answer, and she said nothing more either, being busy with her food. The next course was served. Echo, not bothering with the rest of the silverware, kept right on using the same fork. The corner of the king's mouth twitched. "You are supposed to change utensils between courses," he said.

"I was taught manners, not etiquette," she answered. "I'll switch if you like. Which fork should I use?"

"It doesn't matter," said the king. "That wasn't the one to start with, anyway."

"This will save dishes," Echo remarked pleasantly.

"Unfortunately, now that the things have been set out, I am sure they will wash them anyway," the king told her.

"Maybe they won't set out so many next time," she returned. "One fork is really all I need.

"Have you finished the judging?" she asked, changing the subject.

"Not yet," said the king. "The more difficult cases come at the end."

"Is it interesting?"

"Some of it is."

"I bet yesterday was interesting," she grinned.

The king smiled faintly in return.

They ate the next course in silence, and then the king said abruptly, "There's one thing we had better have clear at the beginning. Don't expect me to give you the moon."

"I don't." Golden-brown eyes met sharp blue ones. "But don't expect me to leave without it."

"If I catch you stealing the moon again, I shall have you thrown back in the dungeons, relation or not," he warned.

"No doubt," said Echo, "if you catch me. But let's not argue about it. We aren't going to agree, so there's no point."

"No?" The king raised his eyebrows. "You don't want to try to settle things, when the moon was the whole reason you came here?"

"If I thought we could... But the purpose of arguing is to make the other person see your point of view. You think the moon should stay in your courtyard. I think it should be returned to the sky. And I don't think either one of us are going to change our minds?" She ended on a faint question. The king shook his head. It was no more than she had expected. "As things stand, then, there is really nothing to be gained by arguing about it."

Dessert was served. Echo, although starting to feel pleasantly full, enjoyed it very much. Sweets were rare in Pebblestone.

"Where are you from?" the king asked, tacitly agreeing to ignore the moon for the time.

"A village by the sea," she answered. "Two months journey from here. At least, it was for me, on foot."

"And what are you, when you are home?"

"I am a storyteller." She spoke with pride.

"Are you a good storyteller?" asked the king.

"Of course," said Echo simply. "I shouldn't go on being a storyteller if I wasn't."

"Tell a story, if you would." It was halfway between a request and a command. "I should like to hear one."

Echo swallowed the last of her dessert and wiped her mouth and hands on the embroidered napkin. "Certainly," she said. And began to spin the tale of the fisherman and his wife: Of the fisherman who caught a talking flounder in the sea but threw it back when the fish begged for its life. Of his wife, who scolded him for his stupidity and told him to ask the flounder for a wish. How, at his wife's instigation, the fisherman asked the flounder for one wish after another, each one grander than the last, first a cottage for his wife, then a castle, then for her to be king, and so forth. The sea was rougher and more threatening each time the fisherman returned to it, but the flounder granted each wish, until finally the fisherman's wife wanted to be a god. When the fisherman returned to his wife this time, he found her sitting in the hut where they had started. And there they lived for the rest of their lives.

There was a short silence after Echo finished. Then, "What does it mean?" the king asked.

Echo reflected that a story didn't have to mean anything; it just was. Or rather, a good story might mean something different to different people. For herself, she liked better the stories in which the meaning was not obvious. If she searched out the meaning for herself, it meant more. But she was also never reluctant to explain things, and this one was clear enough.

"I think that it means you will never be happy, no matter what you have, unless you were happy with what you had in the first place." She continued, almost dreamily, still caught in the thread of the story, "You can ask for the world, but when it's lying there at your feet, you know that even that is not enough and there is as much happiness, or lack thereof, in the meanest hut as in the most opulent palace.

"We carry our happiness inside ourselves," she added. "If we are not happy without things, we will not be happy if we get them. Of course, the fisherman's wife never realized that. She never thought beyond her own desires. Perhaps the simplest thing would be to say this story is an illustration of the fact that the more one has, the more one wants."

"I see," said the king.

Following Peggy back up the stairs to her room, Echo wondered why she had told that story. It was not one of the most entertaining and didn't seem to have anything to do with anything. But it had been the first one to pop into her head and had seemed right at the time.

* * *

Echo spent the next few days learning her way around the castle. She didn't like depending on guides to show her how to get places any more than she liked depending on anyone for anything, so the thing to do was learn the layout of the castle for herself. She walked briskly up corridors and down hallways, looking out of every window she could reach to help orient herself, until she had a fair idea of the location of at least the main rooms, and how to get to them from her room and get back. When she ate supper with the king, as she did nearly every evening, she no longer needed someone to show her how to get to the dining room.

It was while she was wandering around one day that she met her young cousin for the first time. She was turning a corner when a small boy came flying around it and smacked straight into her. "Are you hurt?" asked Echo, at the same time as he said, "I'm sorry. I didn't expect anyone to be here."

Looking down at his tousled hair, Echo was suddenly reminded of her brother, Ralph. Except that this boy was several years younger, only about six or seven, and Ralph, at that age, would never have apologized unless his mother was there to make him.

"Neither did I," said Echo. "You're not hurt, are you?"

"Oh no," said the child. "I ran into a chair, once, and I wasn't hurt then, either. You're not nearly as hard as a chair."

"Why thank you." Echo laughed. "I suppose you must be the prince."

"I am Jonathon," said the boy. "You must be my cousin."

"Yes," she said. "I am Echo."

"I thought you might be younger," said Jonathon. "I guess you're too grown up to play tag?" He looked at her hopefully.

"I would love to play tag," Echo told him, laughing again. "Who's it?"

"I am!" said Jonathon. Echo hiked up her skirts and sprinted down the hallway, and the two of them spent the next half hour shrieking and laughing and running up and down the corridors.

When they were both tired of tag, Jonathon showed Echo the nursery, where they began building a city out of blocks. The nursery was a spacious, sunny room, and the curtains and carpets were bright, cheerful colors. It also had the peaceful feeling that a less busy but well-loved part of a house sometimes does. The cousins worked in silent harmony, the peace of the room stealing through Echo until she felt far away from the rest of the castle and all its troubles.

The sound of the opening door took her by surprise, and she jumped to her feet, scattering blocks. Jonathon also stood up, but more slowly, looking both reluctant and resigned. A lady stepped into the room and smiled at them both. She was tall and graceful, the beautiful white hair piled on her head adding to her height, the string of pearls around her throat adding to her elegance. Her manner was dignified and composed, her dress simple, but of the best material and well-made.

"Time for lunch," she spoke to Jonathon. "Go and wash your hands now. Nurse is bringing food up." She turned to Echo. "You may have lunch with me. I wish to talk with you."

Jonathon, moving to obey, looked back over his shoulder at Echo. "You will come back?"

"I expect so," she smiled at him. "I'll see you later."

"Tomorrow," said the lady. "Follow me," she added to Echo as she turned to leave the room.

Echo followed her a short way down the corridor to another room where a table was spread with food and set with two places. The lady indicated a chair with a graceful motion of her hand. Echo sat, waiting for her hostess to sit as well, before reaching for the food.

"How do you find your room?" asked the lady, as Echo spread butter on a thick slice of bread.

"It is very nice, thank you," Echo began, then struck by a sudden thought she said quickly, "Oh! You must be—"

"The Lady Madelena," said that individual. "And you are Echo, the granddaughter of the forgotten princess."

"Does everyone know who I am?" asked Echo, not particularly pleased. She preferred to think herself invisible.

"Everyone who listens," said Madelena. "You and the Northman between you created quite a stir, you know. First, he refuses to kneel, then you walk up the steps like a visiting dignitary and get taken out a side door—Oh yes, everyone wanted to know who you were and what had been said."

"And you knew...?"

"I know most things that go on in this place."

Echo looked at her closely. "You are not, by chance, another relative?"

Chapter Eight

"No," said Madelena. "On the contrary, I am very much an outsider; or at least I was when I came here. I came with Corinne, Jonathon's mother, when she came as a bride to be married to the king's son. I was her first lady-in-waiting and had been with her since she was only a little girl. When she and Rasmus, her husband, died, I stayed for Jonathon. I also manage the household, so when the king sent a message that his great-niece was to have a place to stay, that message came to me."

"I see," said Echo. "And what did you want to talk to me about?"

"I wanted to see who you were."

Echo laughed. "And did you?"

Madelena smiled, not at all discomposed. "I can see enough.

"So," she added, with the air of one changing the subject, "what are your plans while you are here?"

"Well, I've been trying to figure this place out well enough to find my own way around. And I'd like to see something of Jonathon, now that we've met." She didn't mention that she'd also be figuring out the best way to steal the moon, or, hopefully, meeting Mikkel soon. "You don't mind, do you?"

"Not at all," said Madelena. "Just see to it that he is not

too disappointed when you leave. I would hate to see him embittered the way his grandfather was."

"So would I," said Echo. "But he won't be. He is strong enough to take it. And he has you."

They talked of other things for the rest of the meal. Madelena told Echo about her home, a city some way up the river that had trading connections with Torenia. Echo talked a little about her village by the sea.

"Does Jonathon ever go outside, by the way?" she asked, as she got up to leave. "It seems dull for a child to be cooped up indoors all the time." She could hardly imagine what growing up that way would be like. For her, the outside had always been bigger than the inside.

"There is a very nice garden he is allowed to use," said Madelena with a slight smile.

Echo gave an answering grimace at the "very nice" part. "Well, it has to be better than nothing. Perhaps we can go there when I come visit tomorrow? I'll come earlier in the morning, when it's cool. I could stand to be on the outside of walls for a while myself."

When Madelena directed her and Jonathon to the garden door the next morning, Echo saw that it was even worse than she had expected. The gardens she knew were rough patches of earth, claimed with much hard work from a forest that was always trying to reclaim them. They were planted with sweat, weeded with effort, and had been ploughed with sheer backbreaking labor in the first place. This "garden" was more what she might have called a courtyard. There were beautiful flowers, sure enough, blooming in colorful profusion, with trees for shade, paved stone walks, perfectly cut grass, splashing fountains—and the whole thing surrounded by four walls of solid stone.

"I'm not sure this qualifies as being outside," Echo told Madelena as she stepped through the door. There was not even a bit of bare dirt anywhere.

Madelena smiled. "Is it better than nothing?"

"It will be," said Echo grimly. "Come on," she called to Jonathon, "let's see if we can find any worms."

When Madelena was safely back in the castle, and the door had closed behind her, Echo abandoned the search for worms and marched over to one of the carefully trimmed trees. She broke off a decent sized branch, twisting it loose and wishing for her knife. Once she had the branch, she used it to pry up one of the wide, flat paving stones, loosening it from the ground and then flipping it over to lie on the grass. Brushing off her hands and glowing with satisfaction and effort, she looked around until she spied a small bucket that had been used to water flowers. She dipped it into the fountain and carried it back to her spot of ground, splashing it over the bare dirt. She did this several times, letting the water soak in. "This," she told Jonathon who had been watching with interest, "is mud. You play in it." And tucking her fine skirt out of the way, she sat down on the grass at the edge of the mud puddle and scooped up a handful. His smile slowly widening, Jonathon followed suit.

They were both extremely muddy when they went back inside a few hours later. The nurse, a kindly, grey-haired lady, took one look and sent them to wash up immediately. Echo thought, though, that she was secretly rather amused.

That afternoon, back in her room and in clean clothes, Echo considered a plan of action. The next thing to do, she decided, was to see about getting her knife back. There was no telling when she would need to leave, so it was just as well to be ready.

She had heard nothing from Mikkel yet, but she might any day.

She decided to try by just asking for it. Apparently, everyone knew who she was anyway, so she might as well use it. If that didn't work, she would try something else. Accordingly, she headed for the dungeons. She knew her way around pretty well by now. The guard at the heavy door that separated the underground part of the castle from its more pleasant areas let her pass without comment. She took a deep breath as she started down the steps—and then wished she hadn't. The dungeon had a smell she would just as soon forget.

On her way to the judgement several days ago, she had noticed, on a slightly higher level than the cells themselves, a door that might lead to the head jailer's office. She found it now and knocked firmly. A voice said, "Come in," so she entered and found herself facing the head jailer for the second time. After greeting him politely and receiving a brief nod in return, she said, "I would like my knife back, please."

The head jailer looked at her thoughtfully for a moment and then summoned one of the junior guards. "Calum," he said, "take the princess to the storage room. See that she gets her things."

"Yes sir," said the guard, and turned smartly back to the hallway. "Thank you," Echo called back to the head jailer as she followed Calum.

After all, the head jailer thought, there was no reason not to allow it. His job was to keep the dungeons in the most efficient manner possible and see to it that the prisoners did not escape. He had nothing to do with capturing them, and nothing to do with them after they were released. The fact that the "princess" had been a prisoner was immaterial. She had not escaped. She had been delivered for judgement, had been released, and now presumably had some sort of standing in the castle. So if she came to retrieve her possessions there was no reason why she shouldn't have them. The storage room had a tendency to get too crowded anyway. The head jailer returned to his paperwork.

Calum led the way down another flight of stairs, though still not to the level of the cells, and stopped at a wooden door. He opened it and stood back to allow Echo to go first. She stepped into a large room and looked around. Every wall was lined with shelves, with more shelves in the middle of the room. Chests, trunks, and boxes of every description filled the remaining space. The accumulation of years was stacked on the shelves and piled in the boxes, anything that a prisoner was not allowed to keep with him in the dungeon. Calum went to a group of boxes. "The most recent things are here," he said. "What are you looking for?" Echo described her knife and then helped him look through the boxes. She was the one who found it, eventually, spotting its familiar shape under the pile of strange blades.

She stood up, tucking it into her pocket with a sense of relief. She started to leave, then hesitated a moment, turned back, and asked, "Where are the Northman's things?"

Calum showed her another chest with Mikkel's weapons, topped by the horned helmet, piled up inside. Evidently his armory had been more memorable than her own single blade.

"I would like these as well, if you please," said Echo. She lifted the helmet, a sword, an axe, and no less than five knives of varying shapes and sizes out of the chest. "Could you help me carry them?"

Everything except the battle-axe was sheathed, which made it easier. Echo took the daggers, bundled together in a piece of leather she had found, and let Calum carry the long, heavy sword, the axe, and the helmet. She wasn't sorry to have him with her when she went past the guard at the door again. It made things more official. And by the time they got back to her room, she was extremely grateful for his help. Even the knives got heavy after a while, and all those stairs. And in spite of Calum's presence, she was glad that the corridors were as quiet as usual and that they didn't meet anybody on the way.

Echo nudged the door of her room open with her foot. "Oh, Peggy, I'm glad you're here. Could you take these things from Calum, please? One at a time, just set them down somewhere— yes that works." Disposing of the knives in time to take the axe herself, Echo set it gently down on the carpet next to the other things and missed the look that Peggy and Calum exchanged above her bent head. They had found themselves, on their first meeting, in perfect agreement—this was the most unusual girl either one had ever met.

"Thank you, Calum," said Echo. I really appreciate it. I would have had to have made two trips, myself." She smiled politely as he turned to go, and then, as soon as the door had shut, began looking for an empty cupboard to store the metal in. She found one big enough, ran a finger over the bottom to make sure there was no damp, and stacked Mikkel's things neatly inside. Her own knife, she put with her pack. When her clean clothes had dried, she had folded them tightly and packed them as well, along with a little food. She intended to get more food before she left, but if there was an emergency, her pack was here and ready and she kept fresh water in the skin. And now she had her knife. On second thoughts, she picked it back up and slipped into the deep pocket of her dress. Just in case. You never knew, she might want to cut some more branches.

The next few days passed uneventfully. Echo ate breakfast

alone, lunch with Jonathon, Madelena, and the nurse, and supper with her uncle. She spent part of each day playing with Jonathon or talking to Madelena but still had plenty of time to explore the castle on her own. She was becoming quite familiar with it now, even the more confusing passageways.

It was a week or two after Echo had been released from the dungeons that she met a stableboy as she was exploring the halls one day. This was unusual—not only did she almost never see anyone, but stableboys also never came into the castle at all. Not that it was any of her business and she was about to pass him with a polite nod, when he spoke to her.

"Excuse me, miss," he said. "Someone wants to see you. He said to tell you he came from the north."

"Where?" asked Echo, not keeping the excitement out of her voice. "I mean, I'll see him," she added more calmly.

"Outside," the stableboy told her. "I'll show you." He took her to the ground floor, then to the back of the castle and stopped at a heavy door that could be barred against intruders. "Through there, miss."

"Thank you," she called, already at the door. Pushing it open, she stepped out into the sunshine, hardly noticing it, hardly noticing that she was outside, really outside, for the first time in months, hardly noticing anything at all except that he was there. "Mikkel!" She ran forward and hugged him hard, feeling his arms come around her tightly in return. He lifted her off her feet, spun her around, and then let go and stepped back, laughing. "It is good to be free, yes?"

She looked around then, for the first time, and saw that she was truly outside the castle at last. The small door was hidden in a corner of the building, the place where they stood sheltered by walls on two sides. But in front of them, the grass sloped down to the forest, and beyond that were the mountains, and above them the sky. She could run, if she wished, as fast as possible and as far as she wanted with nothing to stop her. She could walk through the forest. She could climb the mountains. She lifted her face to the sun, laughing too. "Yes," she agreed.

They sat down on the grass, in the sunshine. "How goes it, granddaughter of a princess?" Mikkel asked.

Echo linked her hands over one knee and leaned comfortably back against the cool stone. "Fairly well, I would say. And you? I see you got away all right."

Mikkel raised his eyebrows. "Did you ever have any doubt?"

"Not really." She added dryly, "So long as I don't see a dozen or so guards with drawn swords coming over that hill in the next few minutes."

"I've been here a few days now. I think if they were going to come after me, they already would have." He stretched out his long legs and grinned. "Accidents can happen so easily in the wilderness. They probably think that the stubborn Viking who wouldn't kneel to the king got hurt chopping trees and never made it back to camp. Good riddance, too. His trees always seemed to fall in the most inconvenient directions."

He looked at her in mock seriousness. "I would have gotten in touch with you earlier, only—"

"I know, I know," Echo interrupted. "You had to make sure no one had followed you from the work camp, you had to make sure no one had set up a trap around me, and it's always good to know as much as you can about the situation before doing anything."

He laughed. "Don't forget making friends with the stable-hands. I had to find someone to get into the castle."

It was peaceful in the warm afternoon sunlight. Grasshoppers whirred lazily in the tall grass. A breeze stirred Echo's hair.

"I got your weapons out of the dungeons," she told him. "They're in my room now. I can bring them, at least some of them, next time I come. It may take a few trips. One of the guards helped me carry them up from the dungeon."

"Good girl!" he approved. "I'll be glad to have those back. You've saved me having to find another set, not to mention the sentimental value. I might even have risked going back into the dungeon again, for the axe, if nothing else."

She laughed, then frowned. I'm afraid that Torkel will know I took them. It wasn't exactly a secret. I did think of asking Calum and Peggy not to say anything, but there was the guard at the door as well, and the head jailer, and anyone else who might have seen us. I figured that it was better to let people say what they would than look like I was trying to hide something, and that if Torkel knew anything about you at all he would know that you wouldn't give up till you got the moon."

"It doesn't matter. I suppose you wouldn't have heard—he's gone."

"Gone? Where?"

"Who knows? I heard he left not too long after we were imprisoned. He never stays in one place too long. Maybe he was getting bored. After all, no one had tried to steal the moon in weeks, not after we were locked up."

"Pity he didn't stay longer." She smiled. "He could have had some more excitement.

"Well," she stood up, "I'd better go back in. I'm having supper with my uncle in an hour. When do you want to meet next?"

"How about tomorrow, after supper? The days are still long enough that there will be plenty of light, but the longer shadows will make it easier to get here without being seen."

"All right. I'll bring your precious axe with me."

"And at least one of the daggers," he called after her.

She laughed as she went back through the door.

Three days later, on another long summer evening, Echo pushed open the thick door and stepped out onto the grass. She dumped Mikkel's helmet and three of his knives on the ground. "There you are," she said. "That's the last of it. And how you manage to *wear* all of that, and still fight, I do not understand."

Mikkel straightened up from propping the door open with a chunk of stone. After the first day, they had been careful to do that so no one could come along and bolt it from the inside without their knowing. "It's a gift." He grinned.

"Any ideas for stealing the moon yet?"

"Now that I have my weapons back, I could attack the guards while you—"

"Yes, because that worked so well last time," Echo interrupted.

"You weren't there last time. I had to fight the guards *and* steal the moon. Now I could fight the guards while you steal the moon."

"I still think we need some better ideas. You're supposed to be the expert."

"We'll figure something out." He picked up one of the knives and leaned back against the wall. "There's still time."

"How much?" She sat down across from him.

He took out a whetstone and began running the knife over it. "A few weeks, at least. Not too much more. We wouldn't want to be caught in the mountains when snow falls. Don't worry, Echo. We'll manage it."

"I know we will." She picked a blade of the long grass and

started weaving it through her fingers.

"The most difficult part will be getting the moon out of the city, and then away from it," he said. "Once we're in the mountains, even the forest, we'll be all right. But you can't move very fast with something that heavy, and it would be easy to track."

"We'll figure it out," said Echo. They left the subject of the moon for the time. Mikkel sharpened his knives, while Echo told a story, and the shadows slowly lengthened over the grass.

The story she told was of the man who had never known sorrow or want. There was a king who was gravely ill, and only the shirt from the back of a man who had never known sorrow or want could save him. The king searched for this man, first among the nobles and the richest people in the kingdom, later among the working people and the poor. But all had known sorrow or want at some point. At last, a man was found, sitting in a ditch and whistling, who had never known sorrow or want. But this man did not even own a shirt.

When it was finished, Echo said thoughtfully, "I am not sure about that story. If someone has never been unhappy, can that person ever truly be happy?"

"I would think he would be nothing but happy," Mikkel said. "Happiness is the opposite of unhappiness, so if you are not one, you are the other."

It was a habit they had started in the dungeons, for her to tell a story, and then for them to argue about it.

"But most people experience both. Sorrow teaches us the meaning of happiness, teaches us to appreciate it, to value it. How could he have one without the other? How would he even know whether he was happy or unhappy?"

"That man had obviously experienced things that would

make most people unhappy," Mikkel argued. "There he was sitting in a ditch, whistling. I think he chose happiness, no matter what happened."

"What would happen if he ever *was* unhappy?" asked Echo. "Most of us learn to bear unhappiness when we are young. Little things matter so much to a child—a missed treat, a broken toy, a stubbed toe. But as you grow older, you learn that unhappy things pass, that they don't matter too much, that you can bear them. You learn to overcome things. If someone has never learnt that, would the smallest bit of unhappiness destroy him?"

"But this man *had* borne these things," reiterated Mikkel, "And they had not made him unhappy. He had gone without things, but he had never wanted them. 'He never knew want.'" Mikkel paused for a moment, thinking. "I wonder if that made him rather heartless," he said then. "To understand sorrow, one must have experienced it oneself."

"Yes," agreed Echo. "He would never be able to sympathize with what another person was feeling. He would be alone— alone with his happiness."

"And he would never know it," added Mikkel.

"Ignorance is bliss, or so they say," remarked Echo cheerfully. She knew it was true. Ignorance *was* bliss, but she would never give up knowledge for it. Knowledge is power, and to give up power is no easy thing.

Mikkel finished sharpening a knife, sheathed it, and picked up another one. Echo nudged the helmet. "Does this count as a weapon?" she asked.

Mikkel grinned wickedly. "Probably the way I used it after they had taken everything else made them think that it did."

* * *

At dinner one night, Echo said, "Uncle, I have a favor to ask of you." They got along pretty well by this time. Echo was a good listener, and the king was not sorry to have someone to talk to. She was an outsider, and he could tell her about his worries and cares, matters of state and politics—it didn't matter because she was the only person near him who didn't have an axe to grind. Except in the matter of the moon, but they had agreed to leave that alone. Often, too, Echo would tell stories, making them as entertaining as she could so that the king could laugh, and take his mind off his kingdom for a while. Sometimes she would talk about Pebblestone, about her brother and sister and cousins, and their doings in the village.

"I am still not going to let you take the moon," the king said immediately. "We've been over this. I found it, I brought it to the city, it stays where it is. Anyone who wants to see it can come and look at it here, and it only costs a penny."

"When the moon was in the sky," said Echo, "we could see it for nothing. We had only to look up."

"You are not to ask for the moon," said the king.

"I wasn't going to," she said.

"What?"

"As you said, we've been over this. My favor is for something else entirely."

"Then why were you talking about the moon?" grumbled the king.

"You started it," Echo pointed out.

"What did you want to ask?" Pointedly ignoring the argument, he returned to the original subject.

"There is an old man in the dungeons," said Echo. "He has

been there a very long time. His name is Andrew. Would you set him free?"

The king stared ahead in silence for a few moments. Then he sighed deeply. "All right. I will see to it."

A few days later, Echo saw Andrew released from the dungeons. His son, who had a place some distance from the city, came to take him home.

* * *

Echo ran down to see Mikkel after her conversation with the king, her eyes shining with excitement. "I know how to get the moon out of the city," she said. "We get the king to move it for us."

Mikkel understood immediately, and thought for a moment, his mind going over possibilities. "Can you do that?" he asked.

"I think so. He's already pretty touchy about it. I think if I push him the right way, he might.

"You'll have the leg work to do," she added. "You'll have to find out where he might move it to, and when, and the best place to attack the transport."

"No problem." He laughed. "I think this might work, Echo. I really think it will."

She laughed back at him. "I think so, too."

* * *

Echo spent nearly every morning with Jonathon. They spent a lot of time in the garden, playing hide and seek through the bushes, splashing in the fountains, or sitting on the clipped grass while Echo told stories. She took him with her once to meet Mikkel and introduced them to each other. "This is Jonathon, my cousin," she said, "and this is Mikkel."

Mikkel held out his big, work roughened hand and the child shook it gravely. "How are you?" he said. "It's nice to meet you." Pretty soon, they were both sitting on the grass, looking at Mikkel's collection of knives, and Mikkel was telling Jonathon a hair-raising story to go with each one. Echo was happy to see that they got along so well.

Once, Echo and Jonathon had a picnic in the garden. Echo built a fire on one of the paving stones, having previously hauled enough wood down from the supply in her room, and they cooked and ate their meal in the open air. "This is fun," said Jonathon, licking his fingers. "I've had a lot of fun since you came."

"Have you really?" Echo smiled. "I'm glad."

"You are leaving soon, aren't you?" he asked after a moment.

"Yes." She gave him a straight answer. "I don't belong here."

"I know," he said. "You are always looking out the windows or over the walls."

"You be sure to keep right on having fun just the same, after I'm gone," she told him. "Find someone to be friends with. You can go outside, you know, into the city, maybe, or out the door I showed you. Madelena will help you. Come on," she stood up. "Help me put out the fire?"

Meanwhile, she let it be known through the castle that she was planning to steal the moon. She mentioned it casually to Peggy and knew that the whole castle would hear it in a day or two. Peggy would tell her closest friend, who helped with the cleaning, and she would tell *her* friend, who worked in the kitchen, who would tell her sweetheart, who was a footman, who would tell his friend, who was a page, who would tell his cousin, a guard, and pretty soon all the maids, all the kitchen girls, all the footmen, the pages, the guards, and everyone else would know. The not-princess was news, and so was the moon.

During the meals with her uncle, she dropped casual references to the moon being back in the sky as if it were as good as accomplished. "When the moon is in the sky again... When I go home after returning the moon... When I go back to Pebblestone and the moon is back in the sky..." Not too often, but here and there throughout the conversation as if there could be no doubt.

Then the whispers she had started ran through the castle, until they reached even the king. The captain of the guard came to him one day, to let him know that there was a possible plot to steal the moon. "It's not exactly a plot," said the king. "She told me she was going to. I'm sure she'll try."

"The thing is," the captain hesitated, "everyone I have spoken to believes she can do it."

"She tried once already, didn't she?" the king said, with an assurance he did not quite feel. "Why would it be any different this time? Just tell your men to be vigilant."

"Yes, Sire," said the captain.

"Do you think she can?" asked the king.

* * *

"This Mikkel that you're going to steal the moon with—do you trust him?" Madelena asked. Echo didn't bother to ask how she knew. Madelena would have heard about her getting the weapons, it was no secret that she was planning to steal the moon, and Jonathon would have supplied the name. Madelena was no fool.

"Yes." Echo answered without hesitation. This wasn't

something she had to think about. "In any case," she added, producing an argument that might weigh with other people, "he knows how to return it to the sky."

"How do you know that what he tells you is true?"

"People usually lie because they are afraid of something," Echo said. "Mikkel isn't afraid of anything." She started down the corridor (she had just been leaving the nursery) and then turned back. "Do what you can for Jonathon after I am gone, will you? I know you will anyway, but—I think if anyone can persuade the king to see more of his grandson, you can."

"Really?" Madelena stood quite still. "And how would I do that?"

"You'll think of something. They need each other. And you."

"There's too much loneliness around here," she told Mikkel later. "Not everyone likes it as much as I do."

"What about me?" he asked.

"You like it too. Oh—you meant... Anyway, being with you is almost as good as being alone."

A look she did not completely understand crossed his face. "Being with me could be better than being alone."

He had said it as lightly as she herself had, in that half-teasing, half-serious way they spoke to each other, but for some reason she flushed, and answered rather at random, with a change of subject. "I think the king will be moving the moon soon."

"That's good."

"Yes. How are you doing with figuring out where he's taking it?"

"There are three possible places, different estates at some distance from the city. It has to be somewhere defensible, and with a decent road leading to it, so that narrowed it down a bit.

Here," he cleared a place in the grass and began drawing a map, "this is the city. And here are the estates. Now the best one for us would be this one, to the north, because that leaves us with the least distance to travel. But any of them are far enough away and deep enough in the wilderness that we should be all right. I'll start scouting possible ambush sights tomorrow."

"We're almost ready, then."

"Almost. Will you be sorry to leave?"

"I always knew I wasn't staying long. I suppose I will miss Jonathon, and Peggy, and Madelena, and the nurse, and my uncle. But this place—no. Too many walls."

They sat without talking for a while, watching the colors from the setting sun change the sky, listening to the crickets in the meadow. It was nice, this companionship that went deeper than words. You could be busy with your own thoughts, with no need to explain them unless you wanted to. Sure, if you did want to, of a listener who would understand. The sky changed slowly from blue to gold to orange.

Mikkel stirred. "Here, give me your knife, Echo." She took it out of her pocket and handed it to him. He tested the edge. "I thought so. Do you ever sharpen it?"

"Well, my father gave me a whetstone, but..." She grinned at him. "It still works."

He looked at her in mock exasperation. "I suppose you've been using it to cut wood?"

"Of course. Unlike some people, I have had no occasion to use my knife for fighting."

He took out his whetstone and began sharpening the knife with a practiced hand. "Let's hope you don't have to. A knife fight is not pretty."

"I suppose an axe fight is?"

"Even less so." He grinned back. "But sometimes unavoidable."

"And when that happens, it's good to have a good axe?"

"Exactly."

The next few days were busy ones. Mikkel scouted out possible ambush sites along the different routes the moon was likely to be taken. Echo would run down the stairs after supper in the evenings, and they would go over what needed to be done, Mikkel leaning easily against the wall, keeping an edge on his weapons, Echo sitting cross-legged, leaning forward, her eyes bright, her hands moving, arguing, planning, explaining.

Once the ambush sites were determined, Echo went down first thing in the morning one day, and Mikkel took her to see them. He had acquired two horses from somewhere and was holding their reins and letting them crop at the grass when she came outside. "Can you ride?" he asked.

"Sure," she said. She had never ridden a horse—there were none in Pebblestone—but she was sure she could manage. She petted her horse's nose as she waited for Mikkel to get on so she could see how he went about it, and then she mounted the same way. She and her cousins had ridden the cows from time to time, when she was younger, so it wasn't entirely new to her. At least, if you could call that riding. It had pretty much consisted of sitting on the cows' backs while they went placidly about their grazing. There was no need to steer, and no point, the cows would never listen anyway. When you were tired, you just slid off and walked back to the house. This horse was much higher off the ground than the cows had been. On the other hand, the saddle was a lot easier to stay in and a lot more comfortable than the bare, bony back of a cow.

She watched for a few minutes to see how Mikkel managed his

reins and decided it was pretty straightforward. If you wanted the horse to go left, you pulled the left rein, if you wanted it to go right, you pulled the right one. Her horse seemed pretty well content to follow Mikkel's, anyway.

Once he was sure Echo had her bearings, Mikkel quickened the pace. Echo found trotting unpleasantly jarring, but they soon quickened to a gallop and that was easier. Even so, she held tightly to the saddle without shame, the reins loose in one hand. Once they reached the forest, they had to slow down to a walk and duck under overhanging branches, and she took the reins in both hands again.

It took most of the day. Mikkel showed her each ambush site and what she would have to do. "Once the moon leaves the city, and we know which route it's on, we'll have to get to the site as quickly as possible. Can you manage the ride in the dark?"

Echo nodded. They were riding back now, having seen the last spot.

"Good. I'll leave your horse by the castle so we won't lose any time. Be ready—I'll come for you as soon as I know which way they're going. And you remember how to find the rendezvous once you get clear with the moon?"

It was the last place he had shown her. "I remember," she said.

"That's about all, then. Oh, once you're in position, you may have to wait awhile. The time can seem longer when you're waiting, but don't get worried and go looking for the moon. It'll be along."

"Have you ever known me to worry?" asked Echo placidly.

He laughed in answer.

"Where did you get the horses, by the way?" she wondered.

"They're borrowed. I'll send them back when we're finished,

so long they have the sense to find their own way home."

"Mm hm."

When they got back, she dismounted and walked to the door rather stiffly. It felt odd to be on the ground again after being in the saddle for so long. "See you tomorrow," she called to Mikkel, and hurried up the stairs with just enough time to change before dinner. It was better that her uncle didn't know how she had spent her day.

Chapter Nine

As they were eating supper, she told the king, "Raya made her life a good one." She had talked about Pebblestone from time to time, but this was the first time she had mentioned her grandmother since the first day. "I think she expected you to do the same with yours."

He looked at her. "You are going soon."

"Pretty soon."

"Are you still going to try to steal the moon?

"Try, nothing," said Echo. "I came here for the moon. I'm not leaving without it."

"You can't have the moon," he said.

"I'm not going to keep it. I'm taking it back to the sky."

"It's very well guarded, you know," the king continued. "You couldn't steal it if you tried. You *did* try once and look what happened."

"I'm a stubborn sort of person," said Echo. "And we agreed that there was no point in arguing over this."

"You could stay, you know," said the king in a different tone. "You could be princess."

"You know I can't stay, any more than she could. But it's nice of you to ask me." She smiled at him. "I'm glad I came here. I'm glad I found you and Jonathon."

"I was a child, you know. And she was almost all the family I had."

"I know. But you're not, now. And she isn't, now. I know that when your sister left, she upended your whole world. You were hurt, terribly hurt. I'm not saying that what she did wasn't selfish. Love can make people that way, as well as self-sacrificing. But you have both grown up since then. You stopped needing her a long time ago. And here in this castle, there is a child who needs you. He needs his grandfather." She stood up to go, and then touched his shoulder and added, "The hurt passes. But the love stays. Raya sent me with the medallion. She sent me with her love."

* * *

Echo ran out to meet Mikkel as she had done so many times over the last few weeks. Only this time was a little different. She was dressed differently, for one thing. Instead of the soft, richly colored dresses with the beautiful sleeves she had been wearing lately, she was back in one of her own familiar homespun dresses. She let the heavy door close completely behind her and stepped out into the night. Madelena would see to it that the door got barred. This time, she wouldn't need to get back in. She adjusted the weight of the pack on her shoulders and stroked her horse's nose as she waited for Mikkel. Clouds scudded across the dark sky, blocking out the stars. Wind whipped at her hair. She shivered a little, in spite of the warmth of the night. It looked like there would be a storm later. She hoped it held off long enough for them to do what they needed to do.

She heard the soft thud of hoofbeats on the long grass. Mikkel was coming. She swung onto her own horse and waited. He didn't stop, just waved as he rode by. She kicked her horse into a gallop and followed him toward the forest.

An hour or two later, Echo waited for the moon, perched as comfortably as possible on a branch. When they had reached the ambush site, Mikkel had taken both horses and tied them some distance away from the road, so that they could not make a noise and warn the guards. Echo had climbed a large tree with a thick branch that reached over the road, and Mikkel was hidden in the brush beside it some distance back. The moon was on a heavy cart drawn by two slow-moving draft horses, so she might have a while to wait. Just the driver on the cart, Mikkel had said, one mounted guard, and the rest were on foot. Mikkel was supposed to take care of the guard on horseback first, so that he couldn't catch up to them, or, alternatively, spread the alarm. Echo shifted uncomfortably on the branch. *Why is it*, she wondered, *that adventures always seem to mean being up half the night? And why do I always end up in a tree?*

She was almost half asleep when she heard a noise that did not belong to the night. Alert instantly and listening intently, she distinguished the hoofbeats of horses, the rattle of a cart, and the tramp of guards' feet. She tensed, waiting. The noises came steadily nearer. Suddenly, the night was split by a horrible sound that seemed to come from everywhere at once. Echo grinned to herself. That was Mikkel, and his terrible Viking yell. Immediately afterwards came the clash of weapons and the sound of a fight. Someone shouted, there was the crack of a whip, and the hoofbeats changed to a gallop. She reached into her pack for the knife that Mikkel had lent her (he had said her own wasn't heavy enough) and held it ready, handle downward. She could see the cart dimly now, the driver, and the large dark shape that was the tarped over moon. Crouched on the branch, she waited until the driver was almost underneath her. Then she jumped.

She landed right next to the driver, the knife handle hitting his head with the force of her leap behind it. He slumped over the reins. *Did knocking someone over the head constitute fighting?* she wondered, remembering her dig at Mikkel the other day. *No,* she decided, *not unless they hit back.* Anyway, it wasn't her knife.

The driver definitely wasn't hitting back. Carefully, she put two fingers on his throat to feel for a pulse. Still beating. He wasn't dead, then. She rolled him off the cart, where he tumbled in an inert heap by the roadside, and picked up the reins herself. The shouts and sounds of battle behind her grew fainter as she moved away.

Behind her on the road, Mikkel stood, sword in one hand, axe in the other. He was just about finished here, he decided. Echo should be far enough away by now, and most of these guards weren't going anywhere, at least for a while. He had attacked hard and fast, taking the party by surprise and throwing them into confusion. The darkness had helped, as had the fact that they had no idea how many attackers there were or where they were coming from. Mikkel left the last two guards fighting each other on the mistaken impression that one of them was the enemy and headed back to where he had tied the horses.

He reached the rendezvous point first, the horse he had kept traveling faster than the slow-moving cart. He had already sent Echo's horse home and would send his own as soon as she got here all right. He tied the horse and checked on the ox that he had left picketed here earlier that day. It had been sleeping, but got up when he approached, so he led it to a nearby stream for water. Once they started, they wouldn't be stopping for awhile.

When the ox had finished drinking, Mikkel took it back to the clearing and harnessed it to the cart that he had also brought earlier and left ready. The cart was simply but sturdily made, the two high wheels making it more maneuverable and better suited to rough country than a four-wheeled one. It had high sides to keep the moon from rolling out, and Mikkel had found the smallest possible cart that he thought the moon would still fit in. It was also packed with supplies for the journey ahead, which Mikkel now unloaded. The moon would have to go in first, and then the supplies would need to be packed back in around it.

He was double-checking the harness and making sure the collar fit comfortably on the ox when he heard hoofbeats and the rattle of wheels. "Over here," he called softly to guide her through the dark. The horses and cart came into the clearing a moment later. Echo slid to the ground. "All right?" Mikkel asked, going over to her. "All right," she said.

They both went around to the back of the heavy cart and Mikkel began unfastening the ropes that held the moon in place. "It looks smaller than it should," began Echo doubtfully. "I hope—" she tugged suddenly at the tarp, pulling a corner of it away from the object underneath. A soft, golden-white light shone out. "Good," she said, dropping the tarp. "It would be really annoying at this point to have stolen something that was *not* the moon." She gave Mikkel a hand with the ropes.

Once they had unfastened and untarped the moon, Mikkel backed the oxcart up to the one the moon was on. The uncovered moon gave them light to work by, which helped. Then they rolled it carefully from one cart to the other and tarped it back over. Working as quickly as possible, they packed the supplies tightly around the moon to keep it from shifting and fastened it securely with ropes. They turned Mikkel's horse loose, unhitched the draft horses and turned them loose as well, and were ready to go. Echo took a quick look around the clearing, hoping they hadn't forgotten anything, as they started off.

The cart had a seat across the front for the driver to sit on, but with the ox already hauling the weight of the moon plus all their supplies, Echo and Mikkel walked. They took a road going north with all the speed they could manage. Considering the nature of oxen, it was necessarily slow.

Echo began to giggle suddenly, and Mikkel looked over at her, surprised. "The two of us on the run like this," she explained, trying to hold back her laughter, "looking over our shoulders, hoping not to be caught by our pursuers. It's like we were eloping."

Mikkel grinned. "Not having much experience with eloping, I'd say it's more like escaping after a raid. Only then, I usually took care to have a good ship under my feet and a fair wind behind me."

They walked on. And on. And on. Echo could no longer see the clouds blowing across the sky. The clouds were still there, but they were much thicker now, and they weren't moving. They blocked out the stars so there was no light to see them by. The wind grew colder. She took her cloak out of her pack and fastened it around her shoulders.

They had been walking for hours now. She knew it must be after midnight. Thunder rumbled in the distance, then again, closer. Lightning flashed across the sky. Then it began to rain. With a sigh, she pulled up the hood of her cloak and tucked her hair under it.

The rain grew steadily harder. The thunder and lightning came so close together that it was impossible to tell which flash of lightning belonged to which clap of thunder. The rain was coming down in sheets. *No, Echo decided, sheets implies something gentler. This rain is coming down like a solid wall.* She was soaked to the skin already, the road was running with water and ankle deep in mud, making each step an effort. Echo had to take care not to slip and fall. She was walking next to the cart now, holding onto it to keep her balance, some way behind Mikkel who was still at the ox's head. She waited for the next lightning flash to catch another glimpse of the road ahead. Wading through the road that was fast becoming a river, glad that she was barefoot as her shoes would probably long ago have become lost in this, she caught Mikkel's arm.

"Shouldn't we find somewhere to take shelter?" Echo shouted to make herself heard over the storm.

"No!" Mikkel shouted back. "We need to put some more distance between us and the city, and the rain will wash out our tracks. They will never find us after this. The storm is the best thing that could have happened!"

Well, I can think of a few things I would like better, Echo thought grimly, falling back to her place by the cart. *A hot drink. Dry clothes.* "That's what I get for traveling with a hard-headed Northman," she grumbled. But she knew Mikkel was right. By the time any of the guards got back to tell the king what had happened, she and Mikkel would be long gone with the moon, and no one would know which way they had gone.

They were traveling toward the mountains, and though they had not reached them yet, the road led steadily uphill, while the water rushed down to meet them. The noise of the storm drummed in her ears, the sound of the rain seemed to wash her thoughts away, and her mind became blank except for the effort of putting one foot in front of the other. She was hanging on to the edge of the cart, aware that without that support she would not be able to move at all and would be left behind in the road until the rain washed her away. Mikkel was still at the ox's head, guiding it, keeping all of them moving. One foot and then the other foot, one foot and then the other foot. Keep upright, don't slip, because if she lost her balance now, she would not be able to get back up. The rain came down like something solid, trying to beat her into the earth. The road was endless, the storm was endless, this night was never going to end...

It must have been several hours later when Echo came to herself and realized that they had stopped. The rain was coming down as hard as ever, although the thunder and lightning were less frequent. "Wait here," Mikkel called, and Echo stood there, too numb with weariness to even wonder why. It was still pitch dark, but she knew it had to be near morning.

She waited, and she must have dozed off while standing, because when the ox started moving again, she was jerked suddenly awake. Mikkel had come back and was leading them away from the road. Echo stumbled over grass and around bushes, walking seeming harder than ever after her brief rest. They traveled perhaps another quarter of a mile, the last bit steeply uphill. Looking at her feet, not looking ahead, Echo only realized where they were going when they stopped, and she noticed that the rain was no longer beating down on her. Mikkel had led them to a large overhang, big enough to fit the ox and the cart as well themselves, and shelter from the rain.

She stood there, stupidly, until Mikkel came to where she was standing. "We'll camp here," he said. "I'll unhitch the ox. Get some rest."

Echo could see the exhaustion on his face in the light from one of the receding lighting flashes. She tried to let go of the edge of the cart and realized that she had been clutching it for so long that her hand had no feeling left. She rubbed her stiffened fingers with her other hand until she could unclamp them from the wood and then moved forward and started unfastening the straps on the harness. Mikkel worked at the straps on the other side until they had the ox unharnessed.

Then Mikkel put a hand on her arm. "You're falling over on your feet," he said gently. "Go get some sleep."

This time, Echo made no argument. She stumbled to the side, collapsing on some dry leaves that had collected near the back wall of the overhang, too tired to worry about her wet clothes. Outside, the rain was still pouring down. She was dimly aware of Mikkel rubbing down the ox with a handful of grass that had been growing under the edge of the overhang and was partially dry, but before he had finished, she was asleep.

Mikkel finished making the ox comfortable and tethered it to an outcropping of stone. He glanced over at Echo and smiled a little in spite of his weariness. She had taken off her hood and pulled her hair free of her cloak before she slept. He stretched out in the opposite corner and was soon asleep himself.

* * *

Echo awoke later that day to see sunlight streaming down past the edge of the overhang. She scrambled to her feet and went outside, soaking the warmth into her bones. The sky was a brilliant, cloudless blue, as if there had never been such a thing as a storm in the world. It was a perfectly beautiful fall day.

She looked around to see what sort of place they had come

to. From the overhang, the ground sloped down to a small meadow, surrounded by trees. The ox was cropping grass as contentedly as if winter would never come. Echo could hear the sound of a small stream from behind the trees at the bottom of the meadow. Water, grass, shelter. It was a good place, set far back and hidden from the road. Mikkel had found this spot during the days of preparation and picked it as a camping place.

He was standing just outside the overhang, taking stock of the weather. "No more rain for at least a few days," he told Echo. "Perhaps longer. We can wait for the roads to dry out a bit and then be on our way. Hopefully by that time the search will have died down or at least moved past us. No one else knows where the path to the sky is, so they will have no idea what direction to look in. My guess is that they will have expected us to head for the sea."

That made sense. The guards were almost sure to tell the king that a band of Northmen had stolen the moon. Mikkel, with his battle-axe and horned helmet, was unmistakably one of those fierce raiders. "Sounds like a plan," said Echo. "What's for breakfast?" She turned to the cart, and pulling back the tarp, began to rummage in the bundles packed around the moon. Then she glanced over her shoulder to see that Mikkel was obviously amused by something. "What?" she asked.

"It's the middle of the afternoon," he said, still grinning.

"So?" she retorted. "The first meal of the day is breakfast, and I haven't eaten yet today." She turned back to the cart. "If we are going to be here for a few days, we'll have time to dry out these supplies."

"I'll catch some fish," said Mikkel. "That will make an excellent mid-afternoon meal." He dodged a clump of mud which Echo threw at him.

"I'll make some bread out of the wettest of the flour," she said. "We can use it before it spoils." Rummaging further, she came across her own pack, only slightly damp. She looked down at the clothes she was wearing, half-dried, and stiff and streaked with mud, then fingered a strand of hair. It seemed there was mud in that as well. Taking her pack, she headed towards the sound of water. "I'm going to wash before you start fishing."

"Go downstream," Mikkel called after her. "You'll scare the fish!"

He had a fire going by the time she returned from the stream. He had built it with the driest wood, under a stand of trees to scatter the smoke, and he had more wood stacked nearby to dry in the heat of the flames. Now, he was unfastening the tarp from the wagon to uncover the rest of the supplies. Echo went to help, and together they pulled the tarp from the cart.

The night before, Echo had thought the moon seemed smaller, and now, in the daylight, there was no question. She and Mikkel looked at it for a moment, then at each other in concern. "It's shrinking," he said flatly.

"Maybe—" Echo started, not sure what to say. "Maybe something like the moon isn't meant to be on earth."

"It isn't." He started to turn away.

"Mikkel," she caught his sleeve, "When we return it to the sky, do you think the moon will return to what it was? Is there anything we can do?"

"We can try, *elskling,*" he said.

They both went about their work rather soberly. Echo was wondering what would happen if the moon shrank into nothing before they got it back to the sky. If the whole quest was for nothing after all. Mikkel helped her spread the tarp out on the grass to dry and then headed for the stream to catch some fish. She laid out all the supplies on grass or rocks to dry as well. Some things were wetter than others, but she hoped that nothing was entirely spoiled. Then she placed some stones in the fire to heat and set about mixing up the bread. When the stones were hot enough, she would cook the flat cakes on them.

After a while, Mikkel returned with three decent-sized fish, his hair damp from his own bath. He sat down nearby and began to clean the fish, working in a companionable silence. Before everything was finished cooking, Echo was envying the ox, still happily munching grass. When the food at last was ready, they both ate hungrily.

In spite of her worry over the moon, Echo enjoyed the few days spent by the overhang. The weather was incredibly beautiful, clear skies and sunshine, while the air had that wonderful quality of both warmth and coolness that is felt on the most perfect of fall days. The days were long and peaceful, an interlude, as much hidden from time as this place was hidden from the world.

Mikkel had thoughtfully packed tools and spare parts with the rest of the supplies. He took the time go carefully over both the cart and the harness, repairing, reinforcing, adjusting, making sure everything would stand up to the difficult journey ahead. He also kept them supplied with fish and small game, which Echo cooked for them to eat fresh, or dried and packed in salt (which Mikkel had also had the forethought to bring) for the journey. The more they could forage for, the longer the supplies would last.

Echo swept out the overhang and washed clothes in the stream. She dried out as much of the flour as she could and made bread and hardtack out of the rest. Most of the supplies had dried out pretty well, so she carefully packed everything back up to be ready when they were ready to leave. She tramped through the woods collecting nuts and roots, as another way to help stretch the food. Mikkel noticed that she never wore shoes, and that even when it was cool enough that she needed her cloak, she didn't use the hood. She went bareheaded, barefoot, like a creature of the woods.

All this thought for food made Echo remember the anxious planting that spring. "I wonder how the harvest is going in Pebblestone," she remarked to Mikkel. "I hope they'll have enough to eat this winter."

"You know, when you talk about your home, you sound as if you don't belong there." He had noticed this before.

"I don't," she said simply. "I lived there my whole life, but I never fit in."

"I have traveled all over," said Mikkel, "but I never found a place that fit me. I never worried too much about it, though."

"I came to terms with it a long time ago," she said. "I would rather be myself than be like everyone else. That's true for both of us, isn't it? If we wanted to change, we are strong-willed and self-controlled enough to do that. But we don't really want to."

"You are too much yourself," he told her. "You could never be anything other than what you are."

"Only because I don't want to be."

"That's the thing," explained Mikkel. "You are what you are, and you want to be what you are. You couldn't change because you would never want to. If you wanted to, you wouldn't be yourself. You could try, but it would still be only a false front."

"And neither of us like things that are false."

"Good or bad, not fitting in certainly makes life more interesting. I'll go right on being a square peg in a round hole," he said.

"We laugh at the things that no one else can see," said Echo.

"We don't know everything, *kjære*," he said gently.

She laughed. "We certainly don't."

One of the nice things about her, Mikkel thought, was that she could laugh at herself.

One of Echo's tasks was to take care of the ox. She made sure he was always picketed where he could reach fresh grass and took him to water three times a day. She petted him, and scratched his shoulders and around his horns, and named him Shaggy. "Don't spoil that beast," Mikkel warned. "He has a rough job ahead of him."

"Which is another reason he deserves a little petting now," answered Echo.

All Mikkel would say in Shaggy's favor was that he was less contrary than a camel.

They had to leave the overhang and meadow long before they wanted to. But winter was coming, and they needed to be out of the mountains before snow fell. Also, the moon seemed even smaller than it had a few days ago. So as soon as he thought the road was dry enough to take the cart, Mikkel said it was time to go. They made sure everything was packed neatly and the tarp fastened securely over the moon. Mikkel harnessed Shaggy to the cart. Echo knew that the road ahead would start getting rougher as they climbed into the mountains, so, sighing, she took her shoes out of her pack and reluctantly put them on.

Mikkel watched with a smile. "It's not so bad, Echo," he teased her. "What if you had brought boots!" She threw him a look, and they started off. The long grass was wet with dew, and she was soaked to the waist before they reached the road.

She soon dried in the sun. It made her think of her travel through the forest that spring. And the weather was even more beautiful. She had always thought that fall days were even nicer than spring ones. The air was fresh and invigorating, even though it grew thinner as they climbed higher. And, although she had liked the camp by the stream, she was glad to be moving again. She soaked up the excitement of traveling, of seeing new country every day, of stopping each night in a new place. She had never been in the mountains before, and she loved every minute of it.

They made camp each night before it was quite dark, stopping near a stream whenever possible. Mikkel would catch fish and build a fire, Echo would cook bread over it, the tasks of camping going more quickly with the two of them. They would make sure Shaggy had water and good grass. And Echo would tell stories, or they would talk until the fire burned low.

During the long days of travel, Mikkel filled in the hours by telling her as much of the history of the world as he himself knew and could remember. Echo listened avidly. History seemed to her like stories on a grander scale, more complex, less complete.

"Nothing seems to last very long," she commented, having heard of battles and bravery, treachery and tyranny, the suc-cession of kings, and the rise and fall of several civilizations. "Also, you seem to have paid attention to the unhappier times. I am sure there were plenty of years of peace and prosperity in there."

"There were," agreed Mikkel, "but peace and prosperity don't make memorable stories. The history of a country can be told through its wars. As for nothing lasting," he went on, "that always seems to be the pattern. People build something. They work hard. Things are difficult, so they try to make them better. For a few generations, perhaps more, sometimes less, things *are* better. Life is easy, and people forget. They forget who built what they have, and why. They stop working for things, and things collapse.

"It is true," said Echo thoughtfully, "that people grow stronger under adversity. The more difficult life is, the harder you fight for it."

"Nothing worth having ever comes easy," said Mikkel.

"But I think the opposite is true," she told him. "We place more value on things that are difficult to attain. We usually don't consider something really worth having unless we have had to fight for it. We don't value things that come too easily."

"Maybe that's because it's in our nature never to be satisfied. We need something to fight for, or we would have nothing to live for. If we're not struggling for something, we become complacent, like people when life is too easy. We need something to work for, something to look forward to. They say that where there is life there is hope, but most of us need hope to live."

"We always strive for what we can never attain," she said. "We never get what we want but we never stop trying for it. Is that uplifting or discouraging?"

"That might depend on what sort of person you are," he replied. "You can always hope for something, and maybe the hope is enough. The fight itself is enough, even if you never get what you are fighting for."

"I suppose," she said slowly, "That that is why we were not created perfect—so that we could always try to be."

She laughed, suddenly. "I wonder if we really know anything at all."

"Well," Mikkel grinned, wryly, "we try to make sense of the

universe so we can understand our place in it."

Echo thought that was partly why she liked stories. Stories were reflections of life, simplified, clearer. She knew the end to every story, how everything turned out, what everything led to. In a story, you saw the whole picture, but in life, you saw only your piece of it. Sometimes not even that.

They had left the road, now, and were traveling through wilderness. There was little underbrush, which made things easier, and most of the trees were widely spaced. Sometimes, Mikkel led them around patches of thicker wood, choosing the easiest path for the cart. Progress was necessarily slow. Shaggy's pace was little better than an amble, in spite of Mikkel's best efforts. But the ox was good-tempered and willing, and Echo liked him.

Every day, they climbed higher. Many of the trees were pines now, stretching their tall, pointed tops toward the sky, leaving a thick carpet of needles underfoot. Echo picked up a pinecone and fiddled with it as she walked, slowly breaking off each of the woody, pointed pieces until there was nothing left but the core.

She drank in the beauty of the fall days. The wind, the sunshine, the brief rain showers, the crispness of the air, the deep blue of the sky—she was happy just to be outside for every moment of it. She had always loved fall, and after being in the dungeon, and then the castle, for so long, it seemed even more wonderful.

And still they climbed higher. The ground was rockier now, grass was scarcer. Grain for Shaggy was included in the supplies, and Echo started giving him a little each night and morning. Now there were less trees, more bare rock. She hadn't known that rocks came in so many colors. There were the usual varying shades of gray, but there were also reds and browns and tans and white and once she saw some that looked almost blue.

Dawn came early to the mountains. At the top of the world, the light reached you more quickly. Echo slipped away from the camp early one morning to watch the sun rise. She found a rock to sit on with a good view to the east. In the grey half-light, the world looked gray too, everything dim and indistinct. The early morning air was chilly, and she shivered and pulled her cloak closer around her as she waited for the sun.

When it rose, a blazing orange ball, it flooded the world with color. Shapes were suddenly sharply defined, clear in the morning light. The sky was orange and gold, purple and blue, pink and orange and gold again—she had to keep turning to see everything. The sunrise was so beautiful it took up the whole sky.

She danced back into camp, laughing, feeling as if she was walking on light. "I take it it's a good morning," said Mikkel, tightening the straps on Shaggy's harness.

Echo spun around, stretching her arms, lifting her face to the sky. "Why smile when you can laugh? Why walk when you can dance?" She whirled one more time before going to the cart and rummaging through the packs for some breakfast.

Mikkel fastened the last of the harness in place. He thought that Echo was more full of contradictions than anyone he had ever met. Sometimes, like right now, she was so alive, more alive than anyone he had ever known. And sometimes, when she was dreaming, or thinking of stories, she was so far away as to almost not be there at all. When this happened, he wanted to reach her somehow, to call her back. But he didn't.

They climbed and climbed, higher and higher into the mountains. Each day's travel brought them closer to the sky. How long had it been since they left the castle? Three weeks? Four? She hadn't counted the days. "Four weeks and three days," Mikkel said when she asked him. The air grew ever colder and thinner.

She was glad of her shoes by this time. The surface of the mountain became increasingly rough and rocky as they climbed. Echo guided Shaggy most of the time now, while Mikkel scouted ahead, looking for the smoothest path or landmarks from his great-great grandfather's trip. Or moving rocks to clear a path for the cart. There were a lot of rocks to move. Even with the extra maneuverability that the two large wheels gave it, they couldn't just take the cart over the roughest of the ground. A path had to be cleared for it.

Echo helped with this too, going ahead of Shaggy and hauling some of the smaller rocks out of the way. Shaggy seemed content to follow her even when she didn't walk right at his head. Her hands were rough and cracked by this time, her fingers sore from rubbing against the stones. Her back ached from stooping, her shoulders from lifting. They were all tired at the end of the day.

As she often did when working, Echo used the time to dream. Her hands could stay just as busy when her mind was busy, too. It made the long hours of moving rocks and walking uphill go by more quickly, while, at the same time, she felt less tired. She dreamed up new stories, and relived old ones. She remembered bits of the past, pieces of her childhood, like the time she had once heard a hint of a story that someone had not remembered completely. It was not even an outline, just a few events and a general feeling. She had been intrigued by the story, had wanted to know the whole thing. She had built a partial picture in her head from the pieces she had heard, an idea from the feeling. It had not been until years later that she heard the story in full, and then she had been disappointed. The real story had been nothing like her imaginings. It had been a good story, and she had come to like it. But the fragile thing she had dreamed had disappeared into the reality.

Mikkel was careful to take note of landmarks so that they could take the same way back. Not having to clear rock would make the return trip faster. Sometimes he would stack a small pile of stones where it would be visible, to indicate which direction to go as they returned. As well as climbing higher, they had also drawn closer to the sea. Echo could hear it most of the time now, crashing against the cliffs far below. Once, through a gap in the rocks, she caught a glimpse of it, an endless expanse of water, stretching as far as the eye could see. It made her think of Pebblestone.

The moon was much smaller now than it had been when they left the overhang. It had shrunk day by day and now was not even as high as the edges of the cart. Echo wrapped it in the tarps and packed the supplies they had left tightly around it to keep it from rolling. She and Mikkel were both worried about it, but there was nothing more they could do. They couldn't go any faster than they were going.

The next day, they traveled even closer to the sea. She could see it often now, and there were even times when they were traveling right above it, with a sheer drop downward. The ground was not so rough, now, but at times they had to pick a narrow path between cliffs, or between a cliff and the sea.

The second half of the following day was like that, cliffs rising to the sky on one side, dropping to the sea on the other. Mikkel walked at Shaggy's head, while Echo walked behind the cart to make sure the far wheel didn't go over the edge. Sometimes, when the ledge widened out a bit, she would rejoin Mikkel in the front for a while.

Chapter Ten

They were traveling on a particularly narrow bit of ledge, and Echo was watching the wheel so closely that she didn't take her eyes off it even when the ledge widened out a bit. When the cart stopped, she almost walked into it. "What's the matter?" she asked Mikkel, coming carefully around the cart. "Why are we stopping?"

"We're here," he said.

"Where?" she asked. "Are we camping here?" She looked around. The ledge widened on both sides, out toward the sea and in to the cliffs, making an area large enough to stop safely. It was nearly level, too. Looking at the sky, Echo realized that it was almost dark. She also noticed that after the open space, the ledge didn't seem to go any farther. The cliff dropped straight down to the sea.

"This is it," said Mikkel. "The path to the sky."

"Oh," she said. "We're here." Somehow, the path to the sky had seemed like the other side of the ocean to her, something you know is there, but you never really expect to reach. Other than the fact that the ledge came to an end here, a not too surprising fact considering the terrain, it looked the same as half-a-dozen other slightly wider places they had passed through the last day or so. "Are you sure?" she asked.

"The landmarks were described very carefully," said Mikkel. "Sea on one side, cliff on the other—"

"It's been that way all afternoon," muttered Echo.

"—the path comes to an end, and there is a white rock over your right shoulder," he gestured cheerfully to a spot halfway up the cliff where a section of lighter rock stood out, "half a day's journey from the stunted pine."

"That's your left shoulder," she grinned at him, "and I didn't notice any stunted pine."

"I'm supposed to be facing forward, of course," said Mikkel. "And the pine must have disappeared since my great-great grandfather's day. Also," he took a couple of instruments out of his pack, "I've been using a compass and quadrant. My great-great grandfather was a careful man, and he took note of his position when he was here. I know where we are." He laughed. "As if I would depend on such ambiguous landmarks! There must be a dozen places within half a day's travel that would fit that description."

"I know," she said. "How much of that did you just make up?"

"The stunted pine and right shoulder," he said. "The rest of it might help, it just wouldn't be enough to find this place without better directions."

"So," she looked around, "if we're here, where, exactly, is the path to the sky?"

He motioned to where the cliff appeared to drop straight down to the sea. "Right there," he said.

She went to the edge and looked up, then down. "I was rather afraid of that. I suppose your great-great grandfather did know what he was doing when it came to navigation? You know where we are, but did he?"

"All my family," Mikkel said, "can sail a ship within an inch of where we want it. We learn to read stars before we learn to read books. If he said it was here, it's here."

"Just checking," said Echo.

Mikkel went to the cart and began unharnessing Shaggy. "The ox can't go this way," he said, "so we'll have to carry the moon ourselves. It's small enough now that if we make a sling out of the tarp, we ought to be able to manage it between us."

She went to help and began unwrapping one of the tarps from the moon. It was very small now, but still heavy. She had moved enough rocks lately to know that it would be very heavy to carry for any length of time.

"We'd better eat something before we start," said Mikkel. "It's a long way up."

Neither of them had had anything since noon, anyway, and Echo realized she was hungry. She set out a supper of cold meat and bread on a rock. Mikkel unharnessed Shaggy, but didn't tie him. Echo gave the ox a drink of water from one of the skins, and some grain. Then she and Mikkel ate their own supper.

When they finished, they spread a tarp out on the ground. Mikkel cut out a large rectangle from one side of it. They laid that on the tailgate of the cart and rolled the moon onto the middle of it, then wrapped the tarp lengthwise around the moon and tied it closely, leaving the two long ends to carry it by.

"Ready?" asked Mikkel, pulling one end of the tarp over his shoulders.

"Yes." She did the same with her side. They lifted the moon between them and walked to the edge of the cliff, where they both hesitated for a moment. "I could go first," he said, not looking at her, "and make sure it's all right."

"No," she said. "We'll go together."

He grinned. "If I'm wrong, we'll be on a much shorter path to heaven."

They stepped over the edge.

Echo never saw what she was walking on. But she never looked down. She kept her gaze ahead and upwards, the direction that her feet must go. It was odd, walking on something she couldn't see. She felt a little disoriented at first, almost dizzy, but later, she just felt tired. They had been traveling since early that morning, and it was very late at night now. The weight of the moon dragged on the tarp, and it cut into her shoulders. She had a feeling Mikkel was taking more than his share, but it was still heavy. They climbed endlessly upwards, and the stars shone out above and below and all around them.

It was midnight when they knew they had come high enough. Mikkel held the moon while Echo untied the tarp. They unwrapped the moon and let it go. She bundled the tarp up and tucked it under her arm. They left the moon there in the sky, turning away and taking the long path down without looking back.

It was early morning, although still dark, before they stood on solid ground again. Shaggy was still there, lying down and peacefully chewing his cud, but he got up when he saw them. Mikkel harnessed him, almost stumbling from weariness, Echo helping sleepily. They both climbed up to the seat of the cart and started down the mountain. She fell asleep against Mikkel's shoulder before they had gone very far, not even the nearness of the cliff edge or the jolting of the cart keeping her awake. At some point, Mikkel dozed off as well, while Shaggy ambled unconcernedly and safely down the mountain.

Mikkel roused when it got light. He woke Echo, and they

stopped and made camp. They slept for several hours, traveled the rest of the afternoon, and then slept the night through. By the end of the next day, the forest was in sight.

"It's funny how the way back is never as long as the way there," said Echo as she built the fire.

"We're going downhill now," said Mikkel, "and we don't have to move rocks."

"Still," she said.

Sometime that night, Mikkel woke up. He was lying on his back, and when his eyes opened, he was looking up into the sky. "Echo," he called softly.

Curled in her blankets on the other side of the fire, she stirred, then woke to see the moon shining down from the sky along with the stars. "It looks the same as ever," she said quietly. They watched the sky for a long time.

The journey back was much easier. They were able to ride most of the time, although often it was more comfortable to walk. Once they got partway down the mountains, there was even some late grass for Shaggy again. It was getting colder, but they could build a bigger fire in the evenings. The moon was back in the sky, and there was no longer a need to rush or stay hidden.

Sitting around the fire one evening, Echo told the story of a prince named Mannikin. He had been raised by peasants and didn't know he was really a prince. People laughed at his name, but he realized that it was a funny name, and that he hadn't made it mean anything yet. So he held his anger. He went on a quest (there was a princess involved, of course) and had many adventures before he got where he was going. At one time, when he had no money and was hungry, a fairy in disguise showed him a mountain of gold and told him he could take part of it. Prince Mannikin only took a small piece of gold that fit comfortably in his pocket. Then the fairy showed him lots of people who had tried to take too much of the gold, running back and forth and blindly trying to find the mountain. Eventually, the prince got where he was going, accomplished his quest, and lived happily ever after with the princess.

"I understand why the prince only took a little gold," Mikkel said when she finished. "It wasn't because of his better nature or because he wasn't greedy. It was just sense. He was traveling. He didn't want a lot to carry."

Once out of the mountains, they did not go back towards Torenia. Instead, they headed west, toward the sea. On level ground and without as much of a load, Mikkel even got Shaggy to go a little faster. "I know a longship captain who usually passes by here around this time," he told Echo. "If we can catch him, it will save us a long walk."

An overhanging branch whacked him across the face, and he swore strongly in his own language. Echo laughed. She couldn't understand the words, but the meaning was clear enough. She never used strong language herself, but it always amused her when Mikkel did. Probably, she decided, because he was never really angry. Come to think of it, she never *had* seen him truly angry. She wondered what he would do if he was. Not swear, certainly. He wouldn't waste the energy. He would keep the full force of his anger for whoever had caused it.

"What are you thinking about so hard?" Mikkel asked.

"I was wondering what would make you angry," she said.

He laughed. "Thinking of playing with fire, *elskling*?"

"Certainly not," she said. "Just wondering. I think it would have to be something very big, or else something small, by someone you cared about very much."

"I've never known you to get angry either," he said.

She laughed. "For me it would be lots of little things, and then I would blow up over one that didn't matter at all."

They understood each other so well.

Mikkel and Echo were traveling alongside a creek now, which kept them supplied with both water and fish. The supplies they had brought had held out, so with what they could forage for they had enough to eat for a little while. The trees widened out, and there was more grass between them. When she walked, Echo noticed the ground seemed to be more sand than clay.

"There's the sea," said Mikkel. She looked up and saw it, through a gap in the trees. After another few hours' walk, they were there. The creek they had been following ran into the sea, and the land shelved down to a nice, sandy beach. She was glad to be within the sound of the waves.

Mikkel unhitched Shaggy and Echo picketed him out to graze. They set up camp in the corner made by the creek and the sea. "Nils always gets fresh water here, on his way home," Mikkel said. "He should be along any day, so long as we haven't missed him."

"What if he doesn't come?" Echo asked.

"I figure we'll keep walking," said Mikkel. "But we'll give him a few days first."

It was three days before Echo sighted the longship and ran to tell Mikkel. They waited near the camp as the craft was beached neatly on the sand. Echo could see the men hauling water casks up to the deck, while a few idled about with spears, scanning the shoreline.

"Ahoy the boat!" shouted Mikkel, making a trumpet of his hands.

"Ahoy the land!" someone shouted back. Echo noticed that

the deck of the ship was suddenly surrounded by a wall of shields, and that every man had a sword or spear in his hand. Mikkel stepped out of the trees, into clear view of the ship. "I'm not looking for trouble," he said mildly.

There was a shout of laughter as a red-haired sailor pushed through the encircling wall of shields. "You're always looking for trouble, Mikkel. What are you doing aground?"

"Wandering," said Mikkel laconically.

"You scalawag." The red-haired man leapt over the edge of the boat and splashed through the shallow water to the shore. "Shouting loud enough to wake the dead, and I was only trying to catch forty winks."

"As if you would ever sleep when your ship was landing," grinned Mikkel, stepping forward to meet him. "How blows the wind, Nils?"

The red-haired captain walked up the bank, and the two men clasped forearms in greeting. "Fair enough," he said.

"Sailing home?"

"Before snow flies. Hi!" he shouted to his men. "Get those barrels over here! You'll start filling them up unless you want to drink seawater all the way back to Blue Fjord!"

The sailors, grinning good-naturedly, started unloading the water casks, and Nils turned to resume his conversation with Mikkel.

"Have you room for two more?" Mikkel asked, ignoring the interruption. "Myself, and a passenger as far as Pebblestone."

"There's always room for a friend," Nils said. "Who's the passenger?"

Mikkel motioned at the trees and Echo stepped into the open. "A lady," he said. "Captain Nils, this is Echo. Echo, Captain Nils."

Echo held out her hand. "Nice to meet you," she said.

"Sure, she won't take up much room," said the captain. "You all get your things together. I'd better go make sure those boys are doing a good job." He hurried to the creek, lifted a full water cask, and carried it toward the ship.

The sailors worked swiftly, filling the water casks and returning them to the ship. Mikkel helped, shouting greetings to the men as they worked. Echo unloaded what food was left from the cart and took it down to the beach, along with the tools and Mikkel's other things. She kept her own pack with her. Shaggy looked at her curiously and she stopped to scratch him behind the ears.

Nils approached and looked doubtfully at the ox. "What are you going to do with that?" he asked.

"There are farms nearby," said Echo. "One of them would probably be glad to have him."

Nils sighed and shrugged his shoulders. "What's one more?" he said, and shouted at his men to take apart the cart and build a small pen in the middle of the ship. Mikkel came over with several of the sailors and they began prying boards off the cart. Echo was sorry to see it go, but very happy to be taking Shaggy. She borrowed Mikkel's longest knife and began cutting dry grass so that the ox would have some hay as well as grain to eat on the journey. She piled it on a tarp and made the whole thing into a bundle when she had finished.

By the time she carried her bundle of grass down to the shore, Shaggy following, the men had three sides of a pen ready. They brought the ship lengthwise to the beach and tilted it a little toward land. Mikkel had saved out four of the strongest boards to make a ramp, and he braced these against the ship. Echo guided Shaggy up the ramp and into the pen. The men hastily closed up the fourth side. The ox watched, unconcernedly chewing his cud.

Meanwhile, the water casks had been loaded, as well as the supplies from the beach. Echo took a last look at the shore. The jumbled heap of planks and wheels that remained of the cart, the ring of blackened stones where she had cooked their meals the last few days, and the trampled grass were all that was left.

Nils shouted orders, at the same time putting his shoulder to the heaviest work. Some of sailors shoved the boat out into the water, then sprang aboard as their mates pulled on the oars. The sail went up, and they were underway. Echo stood in the bow of the longship and looked out across the ocean. In a few days, she would be back in Pebblestone. She hadn't really thought about it yet. Going back had been even further away than returning the moon.

"You'll be home soon." Mikkel was beside her.

"What will you do?" she asked.

"I think I will go home, too. It's been a while since I've been there."

She said without looking at him, "Remember how we said that people never get what they want, but they never stop trying for it? I was just thinking, we got the moon, didn't we?"

An expression that was half a smile and half something else crossed his face. "We put it back," he said.

They had a fair wind and a good voyage. Echo kept Shaggy supplied with food and water. Mikkel joined the crew in their work, taking his turn on watch or keeping the sail trimmed. When he wasn't busy, he would yarn with the other sailors. Echo hung on to every word of the stories, adding them to her stock, trading them for a few that the crew hadn't heard. The easy banter and the storytelling had a familiar feel that reminded her of the long evenings by the castle walls. Mikkel was even sharpening a knife. "It looks like someone was cutting grass with this," he remarked.

Echo wasn't going to let that pass. "It must have been Sven," she said, straight-faced.

"It wasn't me!" Sven pretended to be shocked. "I know better than to treat a good knife that way! It was probably Agnar."

Agnar protested that he would never do such a thing, and that Ulf must have done it. Around they went, each blaming another while all the time knowing very well who had cut the grass, until they solemnly agreed that Mikkel must have dulled the knife himself, since no one else would dare to touch Mikkel's knives. Echo was laughing by the time they had finished, but all the Northmen managed to keep straight faces. She was at ease with these friends of Mikkel's.

She enjoyed her time on the ship. She had sometimes been out in her father's fishing boat, but she had never been on a long voyage before. It was an in-between space, like the time in the overhang, with daily tasks to fill the days and no need to worry about the future. And she was glad to be on the water. She had missed the sea, all those months away from it. The weather was beautiful, the air bright and clear, although often cold.

On the morning of the fifth day at sea, Echo looked over the rail and saw her own familiar beach with the cluster of cottages beyond it. Someone had clearly noticed the longship as well, because a small group was gathered to meet it. The people on the beach waited silently, not crowded together, but spread out. They were all men, and they were all armed.

Mikkel was suddenly beside Echo at the rail. "Looks welcoming," he observed.

"It will be alright," said Echo. "They are just being cautious. Longships aren't known for being particularly peaceful, you know."

Nils, at the rudder, looked a question at Mikkel, and Mikkel nodded. Nils pointed the ship toward the beach, and the crew stood by ready to lower the sail. Echo ran to the bow and waved at the group on the shore. "Father!" she called, "Grandfather!"

The ship touched the sand, and she leaped out. Her father detached himself from the group of men and came towards the ship, still wary. "It's all right," said Echo. "They're friends."

Word spread quickly, and the beach was soon crowded. The women and children came out of the hiding places in the forest, the rest of the men from the ambush they had prepared in case there was another longship, or the beach was taken. Echo was engulfed in hugs, first by her mother and father, then by the rest of her family. The crowd was all around her now, shouting, laughing, jostling, and suddenly she wanted to be out of the noise. She hated crowds. She looked around but she couldn't see through all the people around her and she wasn't tall enough to see over their heads. She wormed her way to the edge of the crowd and found Mikkel there. They stood next to each other on the beach.

She noticed that someone had shown the sailors where the well was, and that they were taking on fresh water. Some of the villagers were helping to unload Shaggy. "They'll be leaving in a few minutes," said Mikkel. "We've a long way to go before the weather breaks."

"Couldn't you all stay for supper?" asked Echo. "I haven't thanked Nils or the crew properly for bringing me home."

"I'll do it for you," said Mikkel.

Shaggy ambled peacefully up the beach. The water casks were

being loaded.

Her hand was in his, and their fingers tightened for a moment.

"It was a grand adventure," said Echo. Tears pricked the backs of her eyes, but she smiled so he wouldn't know.

"It was that," said Mikkel. "There's not likely to be a grander one." The last water cask went aboard. "You take care of yourself, Moon-thief."

"Why do you call me that when we say goodbye?"

"Because I called you that when we said hello." He let go of her hand.

And then he was gone. She saw him help run the ship into the water, just another shape mixed in with the rest of the crew. She saw him scramble aboard and help raise the sail. He faced the sea, his hand on a rope.

She stood there on the sand, letting the noise and babble of the crowd wash around her, but for once she was not a million miles away. She was right there, on the beach with an aching emptiness in her heart that was at least partly her own fault.

She turned away from the sea. It was bad luck to watch a ship out of sight.

He had gone, and she had been afraid, afraid to exchange dreams for a reality. Dreams were easier because they were whatever you wanted them to be, and once something is spoken, it loses some of its magic. That was why she had never told any of the stories she made up herself, only repeated those she heard from other people. They had already been put into words. There was nothing to lose. Because, once you had something real, the dream didn't exist anymore. Mikkel had pulled her out of dreamland, made her want to live instead of think, shown her a world wider than her stories. And she had hesitated.

She walked up the beach, surrounded by people, but alone,

as she was always alone. She had always known she was lonely, but today she felt it.

There was music in the village that night, dancing and laughter and feasting. A celebration for the return of the moon and her own return to the village. A fire was burning. Echo watched from the shadows. They would want her to tell the story, but this was one she didn't want to tell. She had never liked being the center of attention anyway. Usually, when she told a story, it was the story people were thinking about, not her. But this was different.

* * *

Life slipped back into its old routine. Echo helped prepare meals and store food for the coming winter. She helped card and spin the wool that would be made into new clothes during the cold months when outside work was difficult. She went to fetch water from the well in the village and listened to the other girls laugh and chatter. She helped harvest potatoes and turnips and other late crops. All the things she had always done, every winter, since she was old enough to start helping.

She loved the work. She always had. It was peaceful, and it mattered. But, somehow, this winter, she seemed to go through it faster. None of the tasks seemed as large as they once had. And the cottage seemed too small. She took outside jobs when she could, feeling a little freer in the open air.

There was plenty of time to think, to take stock of things while she worked. Echo reflected that one way and another, she had had a lot of time to think this year. The lonely journey through the forest, the long months in the dungeon, the journey up the mountains. And now the winter. But there were more things to think about now. So she thought about them, and faced them.

Some people are afraid to be alone. She was afraid not to be. She had been more or less alone her whole life, and she understood loneliness. It held its own kind of freedom. That freedom was what she didn't want to give up.

She had started the bread while she was thinking, and now she set the spoon aside and began to knead, adding a little flour as she went along.

Family was one thing. You stood by them, and they stood by you. You had memories together. You liked and disliked some of the same things. They might know you better than anyone else. But at some point, you left and made your own way. It was natural, expected. And although family was always there, you were your own person.

She finished kneading the bread, covered it and set it on the back of the stove to rise, and went down to the cellar for potatoes.

It was that she was afraid of. Of belonging to someone else and having someone else belonging to her. And when you give your love, you never belong completely to yourself again.

Mikkel saw her, really saw her, as no one else did. She knew that much. He saw all her faults and weaknesses as well as her strengths and goodness. He saw right through her, and, if he loved her at all, he loved all of her.

Her hands, peeling potatoes, slowed. *That's as much as saying that Mikkel is the one for me,* she thought. She resumed the peeling at a furious pace. *You're acting like it was a question in the first place,* she told herself. *But it never was, not from the moment he held out his hand to you in the dungeon, and you took it.*

She put the potatoes on to boil and started to clean her room.

Mikkel and she had gotten along well before, but they hadn't in any way belonged to each other then. They had been almost careful not to interfere with each other. If they were to belong to each other, it would be different. Two such stubbornly strong-willed people would not live together without butting heads from time to time, and two such independent people would find it hard to depend on each other. But with both of them, it would have to be all or nothing because that was the kind of people they were. And nothing was easier. It was why he had gone, and why she had not tried to stop him.

She had been polishing the mirror, but she stopped, now, and stared into it. *I, Echo of Pebblestone, am afraid.* She, who had never truly feared anything. *I have always faced my fears. It doesn't do to be afraid of things.* But she had been. And Mikkel had gone.

She went back to the kitchen and shook some flour onto a platter, began dipping fish into it, ready for frying.

She had too much perspective, she realized. She had never let anything matter too much. She had seen everything through the knowledge of a thousand stories. Everything had happened before and would again. It would all be the same in a hundred years. It was no wonder she had fallen in love without even realizing it.

Phoebe came in and began to set the table. Catriona left the spinning wheel and dished up the potatoes. Echo lifted the last piece of fish from the pan and dropped it onto the platter with the rest. Mark and Ralph came in from working on overhauling the boat, and they all sat down to eat.

They ate the good food hungrily, and between bites chatted about the usual things—the weather, the work, plans for spring. Echo joined in, savoring the warmth and love and conversation, because, although she hadn't said anything, she wouldn't be here in the spring.

She would go away again. She had known this since those days on the longship when she had realized she was going home. There was still so much of the world she hadn't seen. In her mind also, was the thought that she might one day see Mikkel again. If she was wandering, and he was wandering too, they might wander into each other.

Echo spent some time at her grandmother's cottage as well. She never talked about Torenia, and Raya never asked. The nearest she came was to mention the medallion one day when they were carding wool together. "You know that medallion you gave me?" she said. "I don't have it any more."

"I know," said Raya. And that was all.

Sometimes the winter seemed longer than others had, sometimes it seemed to be passing much more quickly. There had been a decent harvest in spite of everything, so no one starved. The villagers had managed to do a fair amount of fishing, in spite of the sudden, unusual storms, and an ocean even less predictable than was customary. There might have been less fish for trading than usual, but there had also been less traders, and they had had thin years before. This one wasn't the worst.

The wool had been carded and spun, new clothes made up. The sheep, at any rate, had not seemed to notice anything unusual with the world. The boats had been cleaned and repaired, ready for spring. Sails were patched and restitched, tanned leather was made into new shoes. Everyone waited for spring.

"I'm going away in the spring," Echo told her mother as they worked in the kitchen one day. "I have to see more of the world."

Catriona's hands, buried to the wrists in soapy water, slowed on the dish they were scrubbing. "I know," she said.

"I never understood the need to wander," Catriona went on, "I never needed to see what's beyond the next hill, over the next stream. And neither did your father, although it runs in his blood. But I do understand that you have to go."

"Thank you, Mother," said Echo. She stood straight but felt tears behind her eyes. They loved each other, of course, but usually they didn't understand each other very well. In this moment, though, they were very alike. Each had her own kind of courage.

Then it was spring. A warm wind took the place of the freezing, biting one, and melted the snow. The first brave flowers poked their heads above ground in sheltered places. Birds began to sing.

Echo dug out her rucksack and went through its contents. Blanket, knife, traps, flint and steel, change of clothing. She had been going barefoot for several days now, and she put her shoes, newly made during the winter, in the pack. Her old pair had been worn to ribbons by the rough stones of the mountains. She took out the shell that Phoebe had given her and fingered it thoughtfully. Then she walked down to the beach and stuck it in the sand. It belonged here. She would take nothing with her that she could not afford to lose. She added what food could be spared and set the pack by her bunk. Tomorrow, she would go.

She wandered outside into the warm, spring sunshine. Glancing up the street, she saw someone walking toward her. Tall, wide-shouldered, moving with the easy, swinging stride of a man used to walking over hills or with the roll of a ship. His horned helmet was slung on his broad back, along with his axe and sword.

For a moment, Echo thought her heart had stopped in her chest, and then she realized that was silly, because it was beating so quickly. And then she was running to him, and she was in his arms.

"Mikkel," she said, her voice muffled in his shirt, "you came back."

"I had to, didn't I?" He was holding her so hard it almost hurt. "You were here."

"Another day and I wouldn't have been. Didn't you make it home?" she asked.

"Yes, we made it," said Mikkel. "Nils, the crew, and I. Only I set out again the next day."

"You walked?"

"All winter." He kissed her, fiercely but gently, then let her go a little so he could see her face, but kept his arms around her. He looked at her seriously. "There's no turning back now, even if we wanted to."

"Maybe I still want to a little bit—" His arms tightened— "but I won't."

"I won't either. Even if I do want to. *Elskling*, this is the next grand adventure."

But she knew, and he knew it too, that it would be so easy, so much easier, even now, for either one of them to walk away. His arms had tightened a moment ago because he didn't want to— and because he did. This was everything. They would belong to each other instead of themselves. It would be the end of one way of life even while it was the beginning of another.

Even now, if one had drawn away, the other would have too. Not without regret, but also not without relief. Neither moved.

Then, at the same moment, he pulled her closer and she tightened her arms around his neck. He bent his head and she lifted her face, and when their lips met again, it was, this time, really, truly, the beginning of forever. And she knew that these things were real, the ground under their feet, the sky over their heads, Mikkel's arms around her... She felt more alive than she had ever been.

"Where were you going, Echo?" he asked her, some time later.

"To see the world," she replied.

"We'll see it together," he said.

* * *

Where does any story truly begin? Echo wondered. *And what story can be said to have ended?* It had been not quite a year since Mikkel had walked halfway across the world through the winter, and she had run to meet him. Not quite a year since their wedding day in the village: since they had started this journey together.

Mikkel climbed up the stones and sat down beside her, putting an arm around her. She nestled into his side and leaned her head on his shoulder. "What have you been doing up here?" he asked.

"Thinking," she said. "Remembering."

"Really? I've been doing some of that myself."

"How'd it go?"

"Not badly. I know how fond you were of Shaggy, and you even manage to get along well with the camels—"

"Molly and Sue," she said.

"Yes. Well, as much fun as all these animals are, we're still going to need a better way to travel soon. Then I got to thinking about that story you told once."

"That's a lot of thinking."

"I've almost finished. I'm going to build us a flying ship." He leaned back against the rock, settling them more comfortably. "How is your thinking going?"

"I'm almost finished," she said. The desert was peaceful and so was the silence. The wind blew gently. The moon and stars shone down from a clear sky. They watched the night together.

Echo looked out over the sand, as if she could see, not only the past, but the future. To the long road that she and Mikkel would walk together. To the places they would see, the adventures they would have, the troubles they would face together. To the children that would be born to them, tall, straight boys, who would be fierce warriors and fine men, strong and beautiful girls, who would laugh, and sing, and cry. Echo would tell stories to her children, and they would tell stories in turn, because stories never truly come to an end. Every story is part of another, and in every ending, there is always a beginning.

About the Author

Malvina Tapley grew up on a small farm in the Midwest. With books, she traveled all around the world—or farther—and through time. She loves books and is never without one, even when simply going to the grocery store. For longer trips, she usually brings at least seven. As may be expected, Malvina spends a lot of time (as much as she can spare from reading and the rest of life) in bookstores and libraries. She has read more than a thousand books—and she reads more every day. *Lit by Stars* is her first novel.

You can contact Malvina Tapley by email at malvinatapley@gmail.com.

You can connect with me on:

🌐 https://sites.google.com/view/malvinatapley

www.ingramcontent.com/pod-product-compliance
Lightning Source LLC
Chambersburg PA
CBHW021156310726

48971CB00002B/661